a PRINCE
of VIETNAM
in KOREA

danee choi

Front cover image: kyuree/Shutterstock

Published by

Leith Media Press

LEITH

ISBN: 978-0-9862137-5-5
Library of Congress Control Number: 2016911020

a PRINCE
of VIETNAM
in KOREA

Based on a true story

Chapter 1

One day, Yoona's cousin had a fantastic story for her.

"Did you know a foreign prince landed on the shores of the kingdom a couple days ago?" said Mina.

"Where is he from?" asked Yoona.

"I heard he came from a distant land to the south in a fleet of a hundred ships," Mina answered.

Yoona traced the outline of a small boat on the ground with her finger. She had never seen an ocean-going ship because the corner of ancient Korea she called home was a long distance from the waters of the sea that surrounded the Korean peninsula on three sides.

"What else did you hear about this foreign prince?" Yoona asked.

"I heard each ship carried a great many treasures from the prince's kingdom."

"But what does this foreign prince want?"

Yoona asked this question in a calm manner but inside she felt a faint fear of the unknown.

Yoona was only sixteen years old but she was already familiar with stories of fierce barbarians from faraway lands invading Korea in the recent past. The mountains and forests that surrounded Yoona's village seemed to go on forever but beyond them lay unknown dangers.

"Oh, that's all I know so far. My father just returned from Kaesong where he had some important business. I'm sure he'll tell me more about this prince after he's had his rest," said Mina.

Mina's father was the governor of the province and was often away taking care of many important things at Kaesong, which was the capital of Korea back in that olden time.

"Well, I have to return home now," said Yoona as she got up.

"Wait, mother wanted to give you something," said Mina. "*Umma,*" Mina cried out as the two girls got up and approached an older woman.

"*Aigoo,*" the woman exclaimed as she hugged both of the girls. Mina's mother was Yoona's aunt from her father's side, so Yoona called her Gomo.

Gomo had a pale complexion, smooth black hair and

eyes that seemed to sparkle. Yoona thought her aunt was the prettiest person she had ever seen.

Sometimes, Yoona's father would compliment Yoona by telling her, "Ah, but I think you do look a bit like Gomo. She is my baby sister, after all."

Mina's mother offered Yoona a cloth sack filled with fruit. "Now Yoona, give these to your father for me. These are Jeju tangerines that Mina's father brought from his trip to Kaesong."

Yoona's eyes grew wide as her aunt pulled out a small orange fruit from the sack and handed it to her to sample. The fruit had a soft yet tough skin and smelled like a sweet flower. The thing looked so orange and so bright in Yoona's hands it might as well have been a precious gem.

Yoona put the fruit inside her pocket to eat on the way back to her home. She gave one final bow to Gomo and waved goodbye to Mina before she turned around and started down the path to her house with the sack of tangerines in her hand.

Chapter 2

Yoona made her way up a winding path. A big hill stood between her home and Mina's house. When she was little, Yoona had imagined the hill to be a large mountain. The climb to the top seemed to take up almost the entire part of a morning.

As Yoona grew older the mountain seemed to grow smaller and the climb to the top easier. Today though, Yoona found herself gasping and her heart racing as she made her way to the top of the hill.

Yoona finally reached the top and looked behind her. Down below was the valley she had just left. A green carpet of rice fields surrounded what looked like a walled town.

The walled town was actually Mina's family home and

it was said to be the biggest estate in the entire province.

The estate had many buildings. There was a building to hold rice and a building that held horses and cattle. There was a building that had smoke coming out of its chimney and servants running in and out carrying food.

One of the buildings even had a roof covered with blue clay tiles. It looked a bit like a giant fish with blue scales. Mina's father often sat inside this tiled-roof building and received important men who came on horseback from all corners of the province to discuss important things.

The farmers of the region also came to the tiled-roof building to settle disputes and matters of the law among themselves. After harvest time the farmers dropped off enough sacks of rice to fill up the entire main courtyard of Mina's home.

Yoona turned around and looked over the valley that was on the other side of the hill.

The valley was a narrow green crack that opened up between the surrounding hills. Almost every single piece of flat land was taken over by rice fields. The farmers of the valley built their houses near the hills in order to save the best land for the crops.

Somewhere among the thatched-roof and mud-walled houses was Yoona's home. It was just a little bigger than the other houses. A wall mostly made of dirt surrounded the place. The dirt wall was not as high as the stone wall that protected Mina's family estate.

Yoona's father was not an important governor like Mina's father and owned only a little bit of land. However, the local farmers respected Yoona's father because he was a wise man who had read many books.

A farmer grew rice on the land Yoona's father owned. After harvest time, the farmer who had ten children would tell Yoona's father, "Teacher, the rains this year were so meager and the crows clever and hungry. So the harvest has been quite poor."

Yoona's father would stroke his scholar's beard and say, "Ah, that is the way of things. Seeing I only have myself and my two daughters to feed, I'll take whatever rice you can spare. After all, those who work the land support everyone else."

The farmer bowed several times as he thanked Yoona's father and handed him a sack of rice that weighed less than a newborn baby.

Yoona remembered the Jeju tangerine she had in her pocket. She pulled out the orange ball. It looked like a rare jewel that had fallen from the sky, almost too precious to eat.

Yoona slowly peeled away the soft skin of the fruit. The pulp inside was like that of no other fruit Yoona had known. It was neither smooth nor firm like a pear or an apple but squishy. Yoona bit directly into the soft pulp.

"*Aya!*" Yoona exclaimed as she almost dropped the tangerine. Her eyes were stinging with the juice of the fruit. The tangerine appeared to have spat back at Yoona for injuring it.

Yoona wiped her eyes and resolved not to get attacked by this strange fruit again. She gingerly peeled away the rest of the skin and managed to tear off a moon-shaped piece of fruit, which she then put into her mouth.

The fruit burst in Yoona's mouth like nothing she had tasted before, novel in sensation and sweetly delicious.

Yoona wondered if the people of Jeju Island ate this fruit every day. What sort of tree did it grow on? Was it a large tree or a small one? Did it blossom in the springtime and were the flowers as fragrant and brightly colored as the fruit?

Yoona imagined a Jeju Island native running up and down a tree like a squirrel and grabbing handfuls of orange fruit. Perhaps this native even had a big bushy tail like a squirrel.

Back in those days Jeju Island was a semi-mythical place to most Koreans. Barely a generation or two ago Jeju Island had been a kingdom with a king and queen and its own customs. Surrounded by the sea and cut off from the mainland, Jeju Island might as well have been a place of the imagination.

Thinking of far-off places turned Yoona's thoughts toward the mysterious prince from a foreign land that Mina had mentioned. She wondered if his land was full of fragrant fruit trees. Why did he sail from his kingdom and land in Korea? Was the prince handsome?

Oh, he must be handsome, thought Yoona. But I suppose he already has a princess that loves him, she concluded. By this time Yoona had reached the bottom of the hill and arrived at her father's house.

Chapter 3

The sliding paper doors of the house were wide open to let in any lazy breezes the summer season stirred up. Yoona's father was inside sitting on the wood floor, hunched over a small writing desk. In his right hand was a writing brush. Spread out before him was a scroll of rice paper.

Yoona's father was a scholar who knew many *hanja* characters. With a few deft movements of his wrist and a writing brush he could fill up a blank scroll with the elegant brushstrokes of Chinese characters.

Many of the local landowning families sent their sons to learn from Yoona's father. But it was a rather meager living, for Yoona's father only received a handful of rice in payment for each boy he taught.

Yoona also learned to write a little from her father. *Hangul*, the native Korean alphabet, hadn't been invented yet, so the characters Yoona was learning were those of hanja. Hanja came from a distant land called the Middle Kingdom, as China was known back in those days.

Yoona was quite happy when she received her lessons because she did not have to exchange a single grain of rice for them.

Yoona's father was also the best storyteller she had ever known. Yoona's father had a colorful story for every hanja character he taught Yoona.

"Now, these brush strokes represent a field, with the farmer taking care of the crops. The four walls surround the field and farmer. And the soldier stands guard over everything," said Yoona's father as he wrote the character for '*guk*' (kingdom).

A certain character would remind Yoona's father of a legend in Chinese history. Yoona along with her younger sister Yuni sat mesmerized as their father told them stories from long ago.

"*Appa*, please tell us a story about Korea," Yoona and her sister often begged their father. Their father's eyes twinkled as he rolled his sleeves and shifted to a comfortable position. Yoona and her sister then knew a wonderful story was coming. The way the girls fidgeted with excitement, one would have thought they were two little hatchlings.

And what wonderful stories their father told the two girls! While we imagine Korea today as one nation (mostly), three kingdoms had existed on the peninsula shortly before Yoona's time.

Further back in time, what existed before the Three Kingdoms Era was more than a dozen little kingdoms and fiefs, each with their own ruler, palace and walled fortresses and armies to defend it all.

There was much going on back in those days. Young princes fought with each other for the hand of a beautiful princess, while other mighty princes managed to unite and rule all the lands within their sight. These mighty princes were in turn defeated by even mightier princes.

There was one story that Yoona always asked her father to re-tell, the story of Hwang-ok:

Hwang-ok was a princess who lived in a faraway kingdom called Ahoda. One day her father had a dream that she was to marry a prince from a land across the seas.

Shortly afterwards Hwang-ok set forth in a fleet of ships filled with treasures and many servants. After a long journey across the waters, she finally landed in a Korean kingdom called Gaya. Now the kingdom of Gaya is no more but back then . . .

***

"Appa, how long ago was that?" Yoona's sister would ask at this point in the story. Yoona's father paused, stroked his beard and looked up, as if he was thinking of a very big number.

"So many years ago that if an acorn was planted back then, it would be a giant tree now," he replied. Yoona and Yuni sat wide-eyed as this fact settled inside their heads.

Their father continued with the story:

***

The kingdom of Gaya was located in the southeastern part of Korea near a river. The prince of Gaya was named Suro. He had the choice to marry any of the highborn maidens in his kingdom, but he had a vision from heaven his beloved would come from across the sea.

One day Prince Suro was on a hilltop with his courtiers. He looked over the ocean that lay beyond the hill and saw something that made his heart leap. Just over the horizon was the fleet of ships carrying Hwang-ok and her treasures. The winds stirred and the ships drifted close to shore.

Suro sent his courtiers to fetch Hwang-ok after she and her retinue made landfall. However, Hwang-ok was raised to be a proper princess and refused to be carried off by strangers.

Suro's courtiers pitched a tent and here Hwang-ok waited. After being informed of his future bride's shyness, a rather impatient Suro mounted his horse and dashed to the tent.

The midday sun was getting hot and Suro's temper grew shorter the closer he got to the tent. "I could have the hand of any fair maiden in the land and this foreign princess makes me wait for her," thought Suro.

Suro finally arrived. He dismounted and stormed inside the tent. Out of respect, Suro made a quick bow to Hwang-ok. Then the two cast their eyes on each other for the first time. Despite her upbringing as a proper princess, Hwang-ok let out a soft "Oh!"

At the same time, Suro's sour mood completely disappeared. It was replaced by an unfamiliar feeling inside Suro. Suro's heart fluttered like a bird inside a cage. Both Suro and Hwang-ok realized, at that exact moment, each was destined for the other and their love was true.

Soon after, Prince Suro and Princess Hwang-ok married. They eventually raised twelve children together and lived to an old age and all of their many descendants know the story of their enduring love.

Yoona had heard the story of Prince Suro and Princess

Hwang-ok many times, but each re-telling had the same effect on her and inspired an odd mix of feelings.

Yoona felt a bit of nostalgia for what she imagined to be a more heroic era than the current one. She felt a little sad that Prince Suro and Hwang-ok lived so long ago and were now gone. Finally, Yoona felt a yearning for something but she could not figure out exactly what.

Chapter 4

"Appa, Gomo gave me some Jeju tangerines to bring home," said Yoona as she stepped inside the sliding doors.

"*Unni!*" A child's voice cried out for Yoona.

A little girl that was seven years younger than Yoona dashed inside the room. Her face was flushed, as if she had been running, and her cotton *hanbok* had splotches of dirt on it. The girl hugged Yoona by the waist and buried her face in Yoona's chest.

"Yuni-*ah*, how did you get so dirty?" asked Yoona as she gently pried herself loose from her sister's grasp.

Yoona brushed the dirt off her sister's hanbok and re-arranged her hair. The girl looked like a smaller version of Yoona. She had a small round face and lips that seemed to be always pouting.

Ever since her mother passed away from a fever a few

years back, Yoona found herself running the day-to-day matters of the household. Every morning she woke up before the sun rose to draw water from the well and she also tended the vegetable garden and fed the chickens that lived in the open space in the middle of the house.

Once a week Yoona took a bundle of dirty laundry to a nearby stream and pounded the clothes with a rock to clean off the dirt. It was hard work but Yoona did not mind because the other mothers and daughters of the village would gather and talk as they washed laundry at the stream.

Sometimes Yoona felt a little shy about going to the stream. Whenever she showed up with a bundle of clothes under her arms, all the mothers exclaimed, "Aigoo, here is Teacher Chang's daughter. Isn't she so pretty?" Yoona blushed because she didn't feel particularly pretty.

Yoona also went into the nearby hills to collect small pieces of wood for the fire. The farmer that tilled Yoona's family land dropped off larger pieces of wood that were needed in the wintertime.

The farmer would also help dig a hole in the ground for the winter *kimchi* during the fall season. Back in those days before refrigerators the Koreans stored salted vegetables in big clay pots and buried the pots in the ground to use during the winter months.

Yoona's biggest challenge though was taking care of her younger sister Yuni, who was always running around like a little mouse and getting into trouble.

Just last week Yuni had waded in the pond behind the house and came home covered in mud. She proudly clutched a frog in her hand and offered it to her older sister. Yoona shuddered at the thought of touching the wet little creature, but she took the frog from Yuni and put it in a clay jar.

Yoona proceeded to strip off Yuni's muddied clothes. As soon as Yoona took the last bit of outer clothing off her sister, Yuni let out a cry of joy and ran out of the house.

"Aya!" exclaimed Yoona as she ran after Yuni.

Yoona chased after her little sister around and around a large tree and then down a dirt path. A village dog joined the chase. Soon, a couple of village children (fully clothed, of course) around Yuni's age joined the merry band.

Yoona finally caught up with her sister and grabbed her. At that moment Yoona tripped and fell. The two girls tumbled together on the ground in one tangled heap of limbs.

By this time a crowd of villagers had gathered. The other children along with the dog scattered into the crowd.

Yoona tidied herself up as best as she could, gave a deep bow to the crowd and hurried back home with Yuni.

Back then it wasn't an unusual sight for a little child to be running around almost naked in a small village but Yoona felt terribly embarrassed. She only gently scolded Yuni for the escapade because she loved her little sister very much, though.

When the two sisters came back home, Yoona's mood brightened because her father was cooking something in the pot. Yoona wondered if it was *samgyetang* because the day had been so hot.

Even back then, Koreans thought the best thing for a hot summer day was an even hotter pot of samgyetang, or boiled chicken. However, it would have been quite a luxury to have an entire chicken in one person's bowl. Rather, an entire chicken was shared among the whole family.

It was time to eat. A fragrant smell of ginseng rose up from the bowl of soup in front of Yoona. Slivers of white meat floated on top of the soup broth. It *was* samgyetang. Both Yoona and her sister tackled their soup with gusto.

"Could you imagine what I found this afternoon? A big frog sitting in one of the pots, as though it was a gift from heaven. It certainly makes a good soup," said Yoona's father. He chuckled and continued with his meal.

Yuni paused with a spoon in her hand. Her face contorted into a funny expression and then turned red. Finally the tears came down like a summer downpour as Yuni cried and cried.

Yoona tried to comfort her sister with a hug. Meanwhile their father smiled as if he was amused at the fickle moods of the females in his household and resumed eating his soup.

The incident with the frog soup was a week ago. Yoona was reminded of it as she cleaned up Yuni. She turned her attention to her father. He was studiously engaged at his writing table.

"Appa, please try some Jeju tangerines," said Yoona as she served the colorful fruits in a bowl. Yuni's eyes grew wide when she saw the exotic fruit.

"Sure, sure," mumbled Yoona's father.

Yoona's father was concentrating on the piece of paper before him. He furrowed his brow, stroked his chin and then dipped his brush in black ink. With a few deft movements of the brush, Yoona's father wrote a couple hanja characters on the sheet of paper.

"Yoona, this character means 'virtue' and this other one means 'patience,'" Yoona's father said. "Note how the very strokes of the character suggest these qualities," he continued.

Yoona nodded, even though she did not really understand what her father was saying. Yoona's father reached for a rolled-up scroll by his side. He slowly unrolled the yellowed paper and ran his finger down a line of text.

"Look here, Yoona. This is our noble family line. Our direct ancestor was a famous scholar who owned many rice fields. He in turn was descended from a prince of one of the old kingdoms of Korea. But this prince was overthrown by another prince who raised a large army and seized the kingdom."

The entire time Yuni had been sneaking up to her father's writing desk on her hands and knees. She was about an arm's length away from the bowl of tangerines. Suddenly, as if springing an ambush, Yuni grabbed a tangerine. She ran to a corner and started to eat the fruit.

Yoona's father ignored the fruit theft and sighed as he looked over the family register.

Yoona thought her father seemed to be touched with a sense of sadness about something lost forever. She came over to her father's side. "Appa, is there anything troubling your mind?" said Yoona as she wiped a bit of dirt off her father's shoulders.

Yoona's father took her soft dove-like hands in his own.

"Yoona-*ya*, one day . . ."

Yoona's father fingered the worn paper of the family register, filled with the names of long-gone noble ancestors.

"Gomo, she certainly married well, didn't she?" continued Yoona's father.

Yoona's father started to roll up the family register. "Yoona, what will I do with you, my poor pretty eldest daughter?" he said.

Yoona gave her father a warm smile, although she did not understand what he was trying to tell her.

Chapter 5

A couple months had gone by since Yoona's first taste of a Jeju tangerine. It was near the end of the summer season.

Yoona and Mina were walking in the hills that overlooked Mina's home. The forest was alive with the sounds of chirping birds and buzzing insects. As the two girls made it over the final crest, Mina's family estate came into view in the valley below them.

The estate was buzzing with an unusual amount of activity.

Porters carried bundles of firewood past the front gates. Carpenters straddled the rooftops of various buildings making repairs. A sharp *thunk thunk* of a hammer hitting a nail echoed into the hills. Straw mats holding fruits and vegetables were laid out on the ground in the courtyards.

"I wanted to tell you, Yoona. We're having visitors in a couple days. They're coming all the way from Kaesong," said Mina.

"Kaesong? That's so far away. I can't even imagine how long such a journey would take."

"And my father told me these visitors come from a foreign land," replied Mina.

Yoona tried hard to imagine a person that wasn't Korean. What sort of clothes did such a person wear? What foods did they eat? Yoona's thoughts turned toward the foreign prince that Mina had mentioned before . . .

"Mina-*ya!*" Gomo was waving to her daughter at the bottom of the hill.

"Yoona, I'll see you in a couple days. We're having a banquet to honor the visitors," said Mina as she made her way down the path to her family home.

The day of the banquet had arrived. It was evening and Yoona was hiking with her family up the hillside path that led to Mina's home. The daylight was fading into twilight. The surrounding trees seemed to cast sinister shadows as the sun dipped into the distant mountains.

Yoona squeezed her father's hand tighter. However the path was narrow and Yoona had to let go whenever she was in danger of losing her footing. Yoona's father carried

Yuni on his back.

Yuni was whimpering, so Yoona's father softly sang a song to quiet her. It was a sentimental sort of song about two lovers trying to cross a mountain pass: *Just as there are many stars in the clear sky, there are also many dreams in our heart.*

For some reason, the song made Yoona feel that aching feeling she had felt before whenever her father told her the story of Hwang-ok. Yoona felt her nose starting to run. Salty tears ran down her cheeks.

"Unni, what's the matter?" said Yuni. She stopped her own whimpering and patted Yoona on the shoulder.

"It's nothing. I just got a little something in my eye. Yuni, look ahead. We're approaching Mina's place," said Yoona.

By this time dusk had settled over the land. From the top of the hill it looked as though a thousand fireflies were gathered in one spot, so numerous were the torches and lamps lighting up Mina's home.

Yoona heard the sounds of laughter and conversation wafting up the valley. She felt cheered by such happy sounds and imagined her sister and father felt the same.

"*Wah*, it's really beautiful," said Yuni as they made their way down the hill.

Yoona, along with her father and sister, finally made it to the front gate.

Yoona smelled the food cooking and felt her mouth water with anticipation of the plates of roasted pork, boiled dumplings and other dishes that would be served. The distinct musical tones of a *gayageum* getting its strings plucked wafted over the walls.

The sounds of numerous conversations seemed to mingle like many streams flowing into one. Yoona thought she heard among the voices a foreign language being spoken as the unfamiliar sounds rose into the night sky like embers in a fire.

Yoona and her family stepped into the main courtyard.

Mina's home was not one big house as we might imagine it to be. Rather, it was a series of courtyards and gardens separated by inner walls, gates and clusters of small buildings. The courtyards were now filled with visiting noble families who had journeyed from all over the province.

"My elder brother and his two darling blossoms have arrived," exclaimed Mina's mother when she spotted Yoona and her family.

Gomo was dressed in a beautiful silk hanbok, with Mina at her side. Her hair was tied into a neat bun and an ornament of precious jade adorned it. Yoona and her sister bowed deeply to their aunt. Mina and her mother returned the gesture to Yoona's father.

Mina's mother and Yoona's father were soon engaged in conversation as the three children stood by their side.

Yoona stared in wonder at the spectacle swirling around them. She had never seen so many strangers gathered together in her entire life. Servants ran around with food and jars of rice wine. Members of extended families were gathered on verandas catching up on news and gossip. Torches flickered and illuminated the scene.

At that moment Yoona saw something that caught her undivided attention.

A group of people dressed in unfamiliar-looking clothing passed by. At first glance they looked somewhat similar to Koreans, perhaps a bit slighter in stature. The newcomers seemed quite foreign in their gestures and bodily movements, though.

What captivated Yoona the most about the foreigners was their speech. It all sounded to Yoona like a babble of rising and falling tones and odd vowel sounds. Yoona had no idea what was being said but she thought the speech of the foreigners was rather pleasant to the ears.

A Korean man approached the foreigners. After exchanging greetings, the foreigners started speaking to the man in Korean. Yoona by this time felt she was under a spell, so great was her astonishment.

Yoona could understand the Korean the foreigners were speaking, although it was voiced with a strange accent. Yoona remembered Mina telling her the foreigners had spend some time in Kaesong before coming to the valley.

As politely as she could, Yoona continued to observe the people from a foreign land.

A household servant approached with a tray of food. "Children, go off and eat some dinner," said Mina's mother.

Yoona had no choice but to follow the servant with her sister and Mina. She turned around and took in one last glance at the foreigners before she entered a dining room.

A knee-high table laid out with dishes was in the middle of the room. A group of children was already seated on the floor and eating. Yoona along with her sister and Mina found an empty spot and sat down.

Yoona marveled at the wonderful variety of Korean foods before her. She was used to a diet of mostly rice and even that was often scarce at her father's house. Spread before her was a range of cooked vegetables, noodles and dumplings.

Another servant came along with an unfamiliar dish that was just recently introduced to Korea: *bulgogi*.

The idea of eating meat in itself was a luxury, but here was an entirely new and exotic dish. The children stared at the thin slices of beef piled on a plate.

Yoona thought the cooked meat gave off a smell that was stronger than chicken but it wasn't unpleasant and made her mouth water. The plate of meat sat untouched as all the children sat looking at it.

The sliding doors of the room opened again.

A Korean boy about the same age as Yoona and Mina stood in the entrance with his hands on his hips and surveyed the scene with his tiny squinting eyes. The boy appeared to be well-fed, with a thick neck, double chin and an enormous belly. A shiny new sword that had hurt no man hung by his side.

Big Choi, as the boy was called, took off his sword and thrust it at a servant that accompanied him. The old man took the sword, gave Big Choi a deep bow and disappeared back outside.

Big Choi made his way to where Yoona was sitting. The wooden floorboards creaked loudly with every step he took. Although Yoona and Mina were sitting next to each other, Big Choi found an opening between the two girls. Without any apologies, Big Choi pushed the girls apart and plopped himself down.

Big Choi grabbed an empty plate and started to grab

handfuls of the bulgogi with his hands. He then proceeded to stuff the meat into his mouth. Between mouthfuls of the food, he offered an origin story for bulgogi.

"This is the way the northern barbarians eat it. We Koreans use cows only for plowing fields, but the northern barbarians eat the meat of the cow as a delicacy. They kill the cow and cut the meat into thin strips and cook it over an open fire."

Big Choi paused and drained a cup of tea. He continued, "These northern barbarians spend most of their life on the back of a horse. They start riding one before even learning to walk."

"And how would you know, you haven't been to the north," said a small child.

"Be quiet in the presence of your elders, insolent brat! I know because my father heard it himself from the King of Korea, who recently sent an army to battle them," said Big Choi. Big Choi was always reminding everyone he was related to the King of Korea through his mother who was the second cousin of the king's third wife.

"An army? Are they trying to invade Korea?" asked Mina.

"Perhaps. The Korean army defeated them because it was just a small force that was sent to spy on our northern defenses. These barbarians have no books or learning but can fight like wolves. They can shoot an arrow backwards while riding a horse at full gallop," said Big Choi as he made a motion to turn his torso around and shoot an invisible bow and arrow.

All the children gasped.

"If they dare to invade our province, I will personally slaughter a hundred of them," said Big Choi as he curled the fat fingers of one hand into a fist. The other hand was stuffing more food into his mouth.

The sliding doors opened again and a servant came in with a fresh plate of bulgogi. Everyone followed Big Choi's example and started to eat the new foreign food.

Yoona managed to get a small piece of meat about the size of her finger. She thought the taste was agreeable and wished she could have more but Big Choi had taken the biggest share.

Yoona and Mina were sitting outside the dining room on a wooden veranda that wrapped itself around the building. Big Choi was seated in the middle and holding a jar of rice wine in his lap.

The three were resting from the meal they had just eaten. The evening had turned into night and the torches flickered into the darkness. The adults in the courtyard were all laughing and drinking heartily.

Big Choi told Yoona and Mina about his father's plan to expand the family estate. He boasted when the estate was finished it would be twice the size of Mina's family estate and have many buildings.

"Next spring we're going to have fifty craftsmen and workers over to start construction," said Big Choi as he made a sweeping gesture with his arm.

In the corner of the courtyard was a small group of the foreigners Yoona had seen earlier.

"Those are the Dai Viet people," said Big Choi.

"Where are they from? My father told me a little bit about them," said Mina.

"My father personally knows the King of Korea and met the foreigners when they first arrived in Korea. I know everything about them," said Big Choi.

"They come from a land that lies far south to us. The sun is so hot down there that rocks melt. Their land receives more rain in one day than we receive in a year. The trees grow fruits as big as a house. In fact, the people of this land live inside the old shells of such a fruit," continued Big Choi.

Both Yoona and Mina looked at Big Choi in wonder. Finally Mina spoke up. "That's not true, I never heard of a fruit as big as a house."

Big Choi drank a mouthful of the rice wine. "Their world is full of strange things such as little men who spend their whole lives in trees."

Both Yoona and Mina who had never seen a monkey laughed at such a notion.

Big Choi laughed and took another drink of the wine. "One of the little men is staying in the king's palace. My father met him. The little man refused to talk to my father and instead jumped all over the rafters of the palace roof. Finally the Prince of Dai Viet called to the little man and he came back down."

"The Prince of Dai Viet?" asked Yoona, feeling her pulse quicken a little. "Is he here tonight?"

"No, he is with his household staff and retainers at Kaesong," said Big Choi.

Yoona felt it all seemed like a big mystery, these foreigners that came from a faraway land.

"Oh, my father! I need to go see him," said Mina. She gave a slight bow to Big Choi and Yoona and hurried off.

Yoona and Big Choi were sitting together alone.

Big Choi moved closer to Yoona. Yoona felt the warmth rising from Big Choi's body, as if he was a giant stone that had been placed in a fire for a while. Little beads of sweat appeared on Big Choi's glistening white forehead. Big Choi took another drink of the rice wine.

"Yoona, as you already know, my family is going to expand our estate next year. And I've been thinking, I should be getting married soon, perhaps in a year or two. Many girls in the province want to marry me, but I've been looking at one girl that I've known for many years."

"Hyejin?" said Yoona, thinking of a quite pretty girl whose father was a local landowner.

"No, it's someone you know quite well."

"Mina?"

"No, you. I think I'll take you as my bride, Yoona." Big Choi set aside the jar of rice wine and made a move as if to kiss Yoona. By this time he was rather drunk and ended up spitting out a mouthful of rice wine on Yoona's hanbok instead of kissing her.

Yoona fell back on her side. "Why, that's something I hadn't been thinking about. I'm only sixteen after all," said Yoona as she tried to wipe her hanbok dry.

Big Choi's face turned red, as if he was mad. "Yoona, the only thing your family has is your father's name. My family is one of the richest in the entire province."

Yoona felt her cheeks turn warm. "That is the rudest thing I've heard in a long time," she cried.

Big Choi made a gesture to grab Yoona. He lost his balance and collapsed face down on the wood planks of the veranda. Big Choi lay motionless.

"Big Choi, are you okay?" asked Yoona.

A loud snoring sound started to rise up from Big Choi.

"Aya," said Yoona as she pushed Big Choi into a more comfortable position. She straightened her clothing and went to look for her father and sister.

Chapter 6

Several days had passed since the night of the feast at Mina's place. When Yoona told her father about Big Choi's proposal to her followed by the spewing of rice wine, Yoona's father stroked his chin and said, "Well, that doesn't sound like a bad idea to me. You and Big Choi."

"Appa!" protested Yoona and she decided to forget the whole matter.

Today, Yoona and Mina were on the hilltop looking over Mina's family estate. Down below, a group of people were assembled with their horses and baggage. The foreign visitors were leaving.

Some of the visitors were staying behind, Mina told Yoona. The King of Korea had asked several of the noble families in the area to shelter the visitors over the winter.

"So they're making Korea their new home for now?" said Yoona.

Mina nodded. Yoona wondered what would make someone leave the only home they had ever known.

The two girls compared each other's harvest for the afternoon. They often went up to the hills to look for ginseng roots and other plants. Yoona's wicker basket was filled with berries and a couple roots. Yoona and Mina said goodbye to each other and made their way back to their respective homes.

As Yoona walked along the path back to her home, she felt carefree and happy in her heart. The rice harvest was going to be good this year, she had heard from the conversation of adults.

The rice fields in the valley below were a golden color. Soon in a couple weeks the farmers would bring in this year's crops. The summer heat hung in the air but autumn was just around the corner.

Yoona rounded a corner and started walking down the hill. She was on her way home.

Yoona found herself approaching the front gate of her house and realized there was a visitor when she saw a horse tied up to a tree near the front gate. Yoona was scared of horses and felt alarmed when she saw the beast was between her and the front gate. She made a wide circle around the horse but it trotted up to her.

Yoona thought the animal looked even more gigantic up close. She felt the horse was staring at her with his big brown eyes. Yoona tried to squeeze past the animal but the horse was now examining her basket.

The horse inserted its dark brown snout into the wicker basket and made snorting sounds. The animal smelled of hay, sweat and dirt.

The horse finally retreated, chewing on something he had snatched from the basket. "Oh," said Yoona to herself as she looked inside the basket and found one of the ginseng roots missing. She quickened her steps and finally made it past the front gates.

Yoona's home did not have many courtyards and buildings like Mina's estate. If a bird was to fly directly overhead, the creature would see just one horizontal rectangle with two vertical rectangles hanging from the sides.

The bird who had passed over many rich homes would think there was scarcely any food to be snatched from such a small place. But he would be tempted to steal a piece of straw from the thatched roof for his nest.

The doors of the main room were closed. Yoona's father

often sat inside this room, writing. Yoona heard the muffled sounds of conversation coming through the doors. She tiptoed through the courtyard and up to the main room.

When she came up to the veranda, Yoona slipped off her straw sandals and crawled like a baby along the wooden platform. She inched her way, stopping every time the wood started to creak.

Yoona finally reached the sliding doors. The doors were wood-framed and covered with rice paper. Yoona found a small hole in the paper and peeked into the room.

Her father was talking to a young man, Yoona guessed after hearing the sound of the visitor's voice. The young man spoke Korean with the same foreign accent Yoona had heard at Mina's place several days ago.

The hole in the paper was quite small, so Yoona could only see the arms and hands of the young man. The young man's hands seemed nicely shaped.

"Unni, what are you doing?" Yuni's voice called out behind Yoona. Yoona was so startled by Yuni that she jumped and fell against the edge of the sliding door. The door popped open and Yoona tumbled into the room.

Yoona felt so embarrassed she rolled herself into a ball after she fell through the door. She went on her knees and gave a deep bow, her forehead touching the floor. Yoona remained in this position until her father spoke up.

"Yoona, perhaps you can prepare us some tea?" asked Yoona's father.

"Yes, appa," said Yoona as she got up. She kept her head down as she exited the room. Yoona ran across the courtyard and into the kitchen.

The kitchen of the house was a dirt-floored room with a fire pit. Jars of rice and other food were stacked against the wall. Yuni watched her sister as she prepared the tea.

"Unni, who is that man? Are you marrying him?" asked Yuni.

"No, no. He's just a visitor," Yoona answered as she blew into the embers of the fire. A small kettle of water and some tea leaves sat nearby.

"Unni, you turned so red when you saw him."

"Oh, I didn't see him. Everything happened so fast and I was so embarrassed." Yoona did see the foreigner's face, just briefly. She thought if she closed her eyes, she could recall certain features: a long face, broad nose, a full head of dark, wavy hair.

All in all, Yoona thought she had the impression the visitor was rather handsome.

The embers glowed and grew hot. Eventually a small flame flared up. Yoona placed the kettle over the fire.

As the water warmed up, Yoona crushed some tea leaves with a small stone and clay bowl. Soon the water started to steam and bubble. Yoona wondered if falling in love was like brewing tea. Warm embers turning into a hot fire.

"And my dear prince, here is a cup of tea to warm your heart," said Yoona to herself as she stirred the leaves into the water.

"Unni, you're strange."

"Yuni, I forgot you were there. I was busy making the tea."

"Unni, I think you like him."

"No, no," Yoona protested.

The tea was finally ready.

"Yuni, do I look okay?" asked Yoona as she picked up a tray with the pot of tea and two cups. Yuni reached over to her sister. She tidied up her hair and straightened her hanbok as Yoona kneeled.

"Yuni, thank you so much," said Yoona. She got up and stepped out of the kitchen with the tea.

Yoona walked across the courtyard. She approached the main room where her father was meeting the foreign visitor. With slow and deliberate motions, Yoona sat the tray down, opened the sliding doors, picked up the tray again and stepped inside. It was a much more dignified entrance than the previous one.

Once inside, Yoona sat the tray down and closed the sliding doors. She picked up the tray and approached her father and the visitor. The only sound was the *swish swish* of Yoona's hanbok as she moved with measured steps. Yoona fixed her gaze on the tray, keeping her head down.

Yoona set the tea cups down on the table, one for her father and one for the visitor. She stirred the tea in the pot. A cloud of warm steam rose up.

Yoona poured the tea into each cup with a swirling motion that resulted in a gentle sloshing sound, as though a miniature brook was flowing inside the tea cups. After Yoona poured the tea, she stood kneeling in front of the two men.

"Prince Lee, this is my eldest daughter Yoona."

The visitor bowed politely.

Yoona had kept her head down but she was able to steal another glance at the visitor. The prince was a young man, perhaps only a few years older than Yoona.

"Ever since her mother passed away, my eldest daughter has been the apple of my eye. We have little to our name but she would make a good match for a noble prince, don't you think?"

Yoona felt her cheeks flush. Her father was usually

buried in his writing and books for days at a time. When he finally had a visitor, Yoona's father talked nonstop and the words flowed like water in a stream.

"Yoona, Prince Lee comes from a foreign land. The King of Korea has welcomed him and his people to our kingdom. He is going to be staying with us over the winter."

Yoona was quite relieved she wasn't holding the tray anymore because at this point it would have jumped out of her hands.

The prince gave Yoona another polite bow. "I am pleased to make your acquaintance," said the prince.

The two men resumed their previous conversation and Yoona exited the room.

Yoona went back to the kitchen and poured some grains on top of a grindstone and slowly turned a wooden handle on the grindstone.

The grindstone was made of two stone wheels stacked on top of each other horizontally. The top stone wheel had a small opening. As the top wheel rotated, grains fell into the opening and ended up between the two stones. The lower stone had an opening on its side from which the ground-up grains poured out.

The ground-up grains were tiny and numerous, like

stars in the sky.

Just as there are many stars in the clear sky, there are also many dreams in our heart, Yoona softly sang to herself. She felt joy in her heart, a feeling that something wonderful was coming into her life.

Chapter 7

Yoona woke up the next morning feeling not very well rested. The previous night her father had given the new visitor the main sleeping room. As a result, Yoona and her sister ended up in one of the side rooms. Yoona had always slept with her sister so she was used to that arrangement.

It was only after the lamps were extinguished and all was quiet that it began. After a few minutes of silence, a snoring sound came from the other room. The sound came through the sliding paper doors loud and clear.

The prince snored in his sleep.

Yoona had tried to cover her ears but she could still hear the sound, a wheezing and rasping noise. Yuni in the meantime slept soundly on the floor right next to Yoona the entire night.

Yoona felt she must have finally fallen asleep because the loud crowing of a rooster in the yard awakened her. Yoona's head was aching and her body felt sore from sleeping on a thin mattress on the hard floor.

After taking care of her personal matters, Yoona spent the morning on chores. She fed the chickens that wandered about the courtyard and drew water from a well and carried it back to the house. She revived the embers in the kitchen to cook the breakfast rice.

Yoona stepped outside to get some vegetables from the garden. The vegetable garden was outside and behind the house walls.

❦

An early morning fog covered the land like a blanket.

"Oh no," exclaimed Yoona as she approached the garden. The visitor's horse was calmly munching on the various vegetables growing in the garden.

"Go, go," Yoona said to the animal as she tried to shoo it away. The horse flicked its tail and continued to nibble away at a plant.

Yoona made her way around the horse's legs to pick the vegetables she wanted. She felt as though she was in a forest. Yoona remembered the story of a local farm boy who got kicked by a horse in the face a year or two ago.

Yoona began to dislike the horse because it was so huge and stupid. She started feeling irritated at the prince from a foreign land who snored and brought this horse over to eat all the vegetables in the garden.

"*Toki*," said Yoona to the horse. "I'm going to call you Toki because you ate the vegetables like a toki." Toki was the Korean word for 'rabbit.'

Yoona finally picked the vegetables she needed. As she made her way out of the garden, Yoona stepped on something soft. A distinct smell of horse manure hit her nose.

Yoona looked at her dirtied straw sandals. She was going to have to take them to the creek later and wash them out. The morning was not coming off to a good start.

Yoona prepared a breakfast of rice and vegetables for the prince and her father. She set the meal in the main room. By now, the morning fog had cleared and the daylight was getting stronger. The house was stirring with the sounds of the other occupants waking up.

Yoona was walking through the courtyard when her father stepped out of his room. Yoona's father looked like an ancient hermit emerging from a cave after years of solitude.

"Appa, did you sleep well?" asked Yoona as she bowed to her father. "Yes, yes," Yoona's father mumbled, still half asleep.

Another door slid open and the prince stepped out, dressed in a simple robe.

Yoona felt a sense of panic. She wasn't sure what form of address was proper for this foreign guest. Yoona bowed without saying a word and retreated to the kitchen.

Yoona sat with her sister in the kitchen eating a bowl of gruel. She was quite tired from the lack of sleep and taking care of the morning chores. Yoona rested her head against the wall and closed her eyes . . .

Yoona was startled awake by the commotion of people talking outside in the courtyard and wondered how long she had been sleeping. The fire she had lit in the morning for the breakfast was reduced to glowing embers. The smell of wood smoke lingered in the air.

Yoona stepped outside to find Big Choi in the courtyard, along with two other local boys. Instead of his sword, Big Choi was carrying a satchel that held paper and writing instruments. The boys were waiting to get tutored by Yoona's father.

"Good morning," said Yoona. "I think my father will be free shortly. He's talking to our visitor right now. Did you know we have the Prince of Dai Viet staying over at our house?"

"I doubt your visitor is the Prince of Dai Viet," said Big Choi.

"What do you mean?"

"I have two princes and a princess of Dai Viet over at my place. *The* Prince of Dai Viet is staying in Kaesong. He has many family members who are all princes and princesses," said Big Choi.

"Oh," said Yoona. "But surely the other princes are as noble and wise as the Prince of Dai Viet?"

"I suppose they're as noble as can be. Like the Koreans, the people of Dai Viet respect the learning and letters of the Chinese. But these visitors to our kingdom come with little riches."

"And why is that?" asked Yoona.

"They were the losing side in a struggle for power in their homeland."

"Where will they go after the winter?"

"To the north, perhaps. The northern frontier of our kingdom is unpopulated and vulnerable to invasion," said Big Choi with an air of importance, as if he was the king's minister.

The door of the main room slid open. Big Choi and the other boys bowed to Yoona's father in respect.

"Have you boys come for your lessons?" said Yoona's father. "Yoona, go practice your hanja. I won't be teaching you today. Yoona, did you know the prince knows many thousands of hanja characters? I think I'll ask him to show you some."

Yoona's father retreated back into the room with the boys. Yoona had hoped to catch up on some sleep but now the day was going to be a long one.

Yoona went to one of the side rooms with Yuni. A small writing desk was in front of her. Yoona prepared a fresh sheet of writing paper and ink. Meanwhile, Yuni busied herself by folding scrap paper into flowers and animals.

Yoona dipped her writing brush in the ink and started to write a few simple characters.

Yoona thought of the prince's horse that ate the vegetables in the garden as she wrote the character for 'horse.' She wrote the character for 'rabbit' when she remembered the nickname she gave the prince's horse. Yoona wrote the character for 'man' but she did not know the one for 'loudly sleeping.'

Yoona had filled up one sheet of writing paper already, so she pulled out a fresh one. Yoona stared at the blank sheet for awhile and then wrote the character for 'heart.'

Yoona stared at the paper again. She had feelings

stirring inside her she couldn't precisely express in hanja or any written language, for that matter.

The doors to the room slid open.

The prince was standing in the doorway. Yoona and her sister gave a formal bow to him. The prince in turn bowed to them.

Yoona was finally seeing the prince in full view, instead of just his hands or face. The prince was dressed in a Korean man's clothes of white cotton trousers and shirt. Yoona thought the foreign prince could pass for a native Korean. The prince looked rather handsome in his new clothes, too.

"I've been requested by your father to instruct you in writing," said the prince.

Yoona thought there was a note of exasperation in the prince's voice but she wasn't sure.

"I hope the little one doesn't require instruction, too," the prince continued as he gestured at Yuni. Yuni looked up from her paper-folding at the prince with a strange expression on her face.

"No? Shall we proceed?" said the prince. "Listen to me and then write down what I say."

The prince cleared his throat and recited a couple lines of classical Chinese poetry. It was a famous and ancient work that reflected on a lost love: *I wish your heart will be like mine, then not in vain for you I pine.*

Yoona pushed back the loose sleeves of her hanbok so both of her forearms were bare. She straightened her back and adopted a posture which she assumed was proper. The writing of hanja was supposed to be a refined pursuit and required a certain poise and grace, Yoona had learned from her father.

Yoona tried hard to remember the hanja characters of the poem.

Yoona took a deep breath and dipped the writing brush in the ink. She knew every stroke had to be perfect. There was no going back and rubbing out a mistake. The paper was white as snow and the ink dark as night.

As Yoona started to write, she glanced at the prince and their eyes met. The prince's face was calm and expressionless. His hair was dark like the ink and wavy like brush strokes on paper.

Yoona's brush hit the paper and soon the blank sheet was filling up with ink.

Perhaps it was from the lack of sleep, but Yoona found it rather hard to get the brush strokes perfect and remember the right characters.

The prince was watching Yoona's every movement. Yoona tried to pretend the prince wasn't there. Yoona's writing brush seemed to tremble slightly in her hands.

Soon the paper scroll was filled with the brush strokes of Chinese characters. The paper was still damp with fresh ink.

The prince took the scroll in his hands. He looked at the characters Yoona wrote with a strange expression, as if he was stung by an insect.

The prince finally spoke up. "Your brushstrokes are too stiff and unrestrained. And many of your characters are improperly formed."

"Well, I can try again," said Yoona.

"What's the use? And why is a girl learning to write?" said the prince.

Yoona sat silently. Her face was expressionless but inside Yoona was trying with all her might to keep her composure. All the little insults from earlier such as the sleepless night and the dirtied sandals were coming back and hitting Yoona like a pile of rocks.

Yuni looked as though she sensed her sister's mood. Her face turned as red as a beet. It was like a cloud turning dark just before a thunderstorm. Soon the tears followed, at first a small trickle and then multiple streams falling down Yuni's cheeks accompanied by loud sobbing.

"Shush, shush," said Yoona as she tried to dry her sister's tears.

The prince sat in silence. Finally he got up without a

word and left the room. The prince closed the sliding door behind him with a *whack* of wood hitting wood.

Oh, thought Yoona as she hugged Yuni and gently rocked back and forth. Yuni was finally settling down, sniffling a little bit here and there.

Yoona felt as though nothing was going her way this morning. Her head was starting to feel dizzy from the lack of sleep. Yoona wondered where the prince had gone off to.

Chapter 8

Yoona stepped out into the courtyard. A couple of chickens were clucking and pecking the dirt. A murmuring of voices came from the main room where Yoona's father was still teaching the other boys. Otherwise, everything was quiet.

Yoona exited the main gate of the house. A rice field ready for harvesting stretched in front of the gate and a narrow dirt path ran along the sides of the house walls. Yoona walked along the path.

Yoona heard a slapping sound coming from the rear of the house, as if someone was hitting a tree with a stick. She turned a corner and found the prince at the back of the house.

The prince was swinging a long bamboo stick as if it

was a sword.

Whack! The prince hit a bamboo tree that was still standing. *Whack!* The prince hit a bush and knocked off a couple leaves. Yoona bit her lip. The bush had been planted by her mother before she passed away.

Whack! The prince took another swing at the bush as though it was an enemy.

"Please, you're going to destroy it," Yoona finally spoke up, trying her hardest to remain calm. It had been a very frantic morning.

"Oh, I didn't see you," said the prince as he lowered the bamboo stick. The prince's face was flushed, as though he was deeply agitated inside. He gave a courtly bow to Yoona.

"I apologize for damaging your family's shrubbery."

"Well, that's okay," said Yoona as she gathered up the branches broken off by the prince.

"There's been many things on my mind lately," said the prince.

"Perhaps one day you can tell me what ails you," said Yoona.

"I suppose so," said the prince.

Yoona gave the prince a smile and the prince's face seemed to soften. For the first time since Yoona met him, the prince smiled at her.

The back of the house was secluded. Shade trees filtered the sunlight so that light and shadow danced like the spots of a leopard. Beyond the trees the forested hills seemed to go on and on. Yoona felt as though only she and the prince were alone in the entire world. She felt that odd feeling in her heart again.

The quiet moment was broken up by voices and the rustling of grass. Big Choi and the other boys emerged from behind the house walls.

"So this is where the loud noise was coming from," said Big Choi.

Big Choi looked at the bamboo stick in the prince's hands.

"Prince Lee, you hold that stick the way a gentleman carries a sword," said Big Choi as he picked up a piece of bamboo on the ground. "I challenge you then, as one gentleman to another."

"I have no wish to engage in . . ."

Before the prince could finish, Big Choi let out a battle cry and slashed at the prince with his bamboo stick. The prince responded with a blocking motion with his bamboo stick.

Big Choi continued to slash at the prince. The other boys cheered on Big Choi as the cracking sounds of bamboo hitting bamboo echoed in the air.

A duel was underway but it was rather one-sided. Big Choi made wild and frantic motions but got few if any hits on the prince.

The prince in the meantime was quite skilled in his swordsmanship, as if he had trained for many years back in his native land. His movements were graceful. With the slightest movement of his weapon, the prince deflected Big Choi's attacks.

Clack! Clack!

Big Choi's face turned bright red as he breathed rapidly. Suddenly, he threw his bamboo stick aside and rushed the prince.

The prince dropped his bamboo stick with surprise as Big Choi charged him like a bull. The other boys cheered on Big Choi. The two ended up tumbling on the ground.

"Please . . ." Yoona tried to raise her voice but it got lost in the din.

At that moment, Yoona wondered, where was the noble prince she had expected to meet? The prince seemed displeased at helping Yoona with her studies. His horse had eaten the vegetables in the garden. The prince *snored* in his sleep.

And now the prince and Big Choi were rolling in the dirt, fighting each other like two boys.

"Hrrrmp!"

The sound of an older man clearing his throat broke through the commotion.

The fighting immediately stopped. All the children and the prince stood up straight and bowed to Yoona's father, who had made his way to the back of the house. Yuni was by her father's side.

Yoona's father surveyed the scene. The prince and Big Choi were scraped up and bruised and their clothes dirtied. The two bowed their heads and stared at the ground in front of them.

"Well everyone, it's afternoon now. I believe it is time now for tea. Yoona's aunt just dropped off the most delicious red bean cakes," said Yoona's father.

Everyone took the hint from Yoona's father. The prince and the boys bowed in unison to him and scrambled to rush back inside the house. Yuni followed the boys. Yoona turned on her heels to go back inside too, when her father called out to her.

"Yoona, stay here," said her father.

Yoona tried to hide her disappointment as she watched everyone else disappear behind the house walls.

Yoona's father took her hand in his own and started down the narrow dirt path that went up the hill behind the house. The path sloped gently as it snaked across the face of the hill. Ancient pine trees with white bark shaded and sheltered the path.

"Yoona, you are young and there are many things in the world that you may not understand yet," said Yoona's father.

The two made their way up the hill. Occasionally, the trees along the path would open up and Yoona spotted a farmer working in the fields below.

Yoona's father stopped and picked a mountain flower.

"Yoona, it is in the hearts of men to desire pretty things. Because a pretty thing brings joy. At the same time, it can bring pain and much heartache," said Yoona's father as he held the flower up to his nose.

Yoona wondered how in the world a flower could bring pain and heartache.

Yoona and her father continued up the hill.

Yoona looked back. In the distance was the hill that she and Mina often climbed to look for roots and berries. The valley floor below was the golden color of harvest-ready rice. A gentle breeze carried the scent of pine needles through the air.

Finally, the two reached their destination.

The path opened up to a large clearing. A border of trees surrounded the open space. An exposed rock face served as a protective backdrop for a small shelter made of wood.

Inside the shelter was a stone statue of the Enlightened One.

Yoona's father approached the Enlightened One with measured steps and stopped in front of the wooden shelter.

Yoona made her way to her father's side. She saw that her father had his hands clasped together and his eyes closed. Yoona closed her eyes and clasped her hands together in the same manner.

Yoona wondered if she was supposed to feel enlightenment fill her body as she closed her eyes and clasped her hands. She could hear the rustling of the trees. A nearby bird chirped and cicadas droned somewhere. A soft breeze blew against Yoona's cheeks.

Yoona opened her eyes halfway. The Enlightened One sat peacefully in the lotus position underneath his shelter. At his feet were various offerings left by others such as flowers and bowls of uncooked rice.

Yoona knew that the Enlightened One had lived hundreds of years ago in a faraway kingdom. The Enlightened One was a prince and had all the riches in the world but found his life was wanting. He eventually gave up his wealth and spent the rest of his life wandering, searching for enlightenment.

The stone statute of the prince looked quite serene to

Yoona, as if the wandering prince had finally found what he was seeking.

Yoona's thoughts then turned to another wandering prince, a prince who was not made of stone and very much alive and breathing. She felt a rising in her chest, a feeling that was at once both uncomfortable and strange. The feeling certainly wasn't enlightenment, Yoona thought as she looked at the peaceful face of the stone statue.

Yoona closed her eyes again. She tried to meditate on the Enlightened One's teachings as her father had taught her.

Yoona found herself thinking about the mountain spirits. The Koreans back then imagined spirits were everywhere in nature, even in the smallest stone. To Yoona, the spirits seemed as real as the sun shining on her face and the breath in her lungs.

Yoona thought about many things. She wondered if the mountain spirits or the Enlightened One knew of her wishes and dreams.

Yoona thought of everyone else down below in the house feasting on red bean cakes. She hoped there would be a piece or two remaining for her. Yoona heard her father moving from his position and opened her eyes.

Yoona's father was done his meditation. He took

Yoona's hand in his own and the two made their way down the hill.

Chapter 9

Yoona sat with her sister on a straw mat under a tree mending baskets. The task involved taking strips of tough straw and weaving them over the holes in a basket. It was work that was slow paced and not hard at all. And Yoona enjoyed spending the quiet time with her sister.

The trees in the valley were bursting with fall colors in various shades of red and orange. The muggy hotness of summer had given way to the mild days of fall.

The harvesting season had arrived. The farmers in their straw hats were bent over the ground, sickles in hand. The rice fields that were flooded in the summer were now dry.

"Unni, I think it's time for the water again," said Yuni.

A large bucket of water and a ladle sat near Yoona. Yoona and her sister hoisted the bucket with a bamboo stick and went out into the field. They were greeted by the farmers, who took turns taking scoops of the drinking water.

"Aigoo, such pretty girls shouldn't be out in the sun," one of the farmers' wives said to Yoona and her sister.

After all the farmers took a drink the bucket was light enough for Yoona to carry on her own. Yoona took the remaining water to the far end of the field.

The prince was busy clearing land that belonged to Yoona's father for next year's planting. The plot had never been farmed before and was covered with brush and trees.

Yoona's father never worked out in the fields, so Yoona was surprised to see the prince working outside like a farmer. She wondered if the prince really was a prince.

Yoona had imagined a prince to be a royal sort of being who rode a chariot pulled by a team of magnificent white horses. A prince would be dressed in the finest silks and shiniest armor.

The prince had rigged a harness to his horse and was using him to pull a stump from the ground. The prince himself was dressed in the simple white cotton trousers and shirt of a farmer.

The horse strained against his harness. The harness in turn was tied to a tree stump. Chopped-up roots and branches were scattered on the ground. The prince was gently encouraging the horse in his native tongue.

"*Di! Di!*" the prince called to the horse.

Yoona approached with her head down. When she got close, the prince gave another command to Toki and the horse stopped his labor, causing the stump to settle back into the ground like a giant stone.

Yoona silently offered the water bucket to the prince. The prince nodded and scooped out a drink of water with the ladle.

Every day for the past week Yoona had repeated this ritual with the prince. Yoona silently offered water, the prince took it without a word.

It was as though the prince was still embarrassed by the memory of his scuffle with Big Choi. The prince might have been wearing the clothes of a farmer but he certainly carried himself with a noble air, thought Yoona.

After the prince had his fill of the water, Yoona made her way across the fields and back to the house.

Yoona and her sister had mended enough straw baskets and sandals and this task was done for the day. Yoona went inside the house to tidy things up.

It was quiet and peaceful behind the walls that protected the house. Yoona's father was gone, visiting

Yoona's aunt. Yuni was outside somewhere. The smell of burnt firewood drifted from the kitchen.

Yoona picked up a straw broom and began sweeping the wooden veranda that faced the inner courtyard.

Swish, swish. The broom went over the wooden planks. Yoona found herself next to the prince's room. She paused and then slowly slid open the wood-framed paper door.

Yoona stepped inside and swept the broom over the floor of the room. She looked around the place. It was a simple and bare room, furnished with a writing desk, a large wooden chest and a smaller chest. A cotton futon used for sleeping was folded up on the floor.

Yoona imagined the prince didn't realize it was Korean custom to store the futon inside the large chest. She gathered up the futon in her arms and opened the chest. What she saw inside the chest made Yoona gasp.

Inside the chest was a folded silk robe. It seemed to shimmer like the plumage of an exotic bird and the patterns on it were wonderful and ornate. Also lying inside the chest was a sword sheathed in a lacquered scabbard.

An unstrung bow and a quiver of arrows was next to the sword. A military helmet rounded out the arsenal. The metal shell of the helmet was scuffed and dented, as if it had seen heavy use.

Yoona had never seen such weapons of war before. The sword was slightly unsheathed and the glint of bare metal revealed itself. Yoona gingerly reached into the chest and made a motion to touch the sword.

Yoona drew her hand back at the last second. She imagined the sword would cut her finger off. Yoona looked at the weapons before her and wondered what fierce battles they had seen.

Yoona closed the chest. She noticed how plain the chest looked, just pieces of wood held together with iron trim work. Yet inside the ordinary chest was something extraordinary, thought Yoona.

Yoona resumed cleaning up the room. She dusted off the writing desk and the two chests and tucked the futon away in the corner.

Ah my prince, how did you end up so far from your native land, thought Yoona. She finished cleaning and exited the room.

Chapter 10

The fall harvest was exceptionally bountiful. The fields were now bare dirt but every household had a well-stocked larder. It was time for the annual harvest festival.

The rhythmic sound of drums echoed up the valley as groups of farmers with drums and gongs paraded through the village. The villagers visited the tombs of their ancestors in the hills and afterwards played games and feasted for a couple days.

Today Yoona was on the path to Mina's estate. The surrounding mountains were aflame with the ochre shades of autumn. The trees were already starting to drop their leaves, one by one. Little black squirrels ran up and down the trees, squeaking and gathering up nuts.

Yoona shivered a little as the breeze picked up. She

thought about how the winds coming from the north would blow colder as the days went by. The splendid days of a Korean autumn would soon just be a memory and many dark winter days would pass until springtime.

Yoona made her way down the hill.

Mina's family estate came into view. The place seemed even busier than during the summer festivities. Farmers carrying loads of rice and produce passed in a steady procession through the front gates. Yoona followed the farmers past the gates and into the main courtyard.

Yoona felt as though she had entered a beehive. The courtyard was filling up with sacks of rice dropped off by the farmers. Black crows cawed and flapped their wings overhead, trying to catch stray grains spilled on the ground.

An important-looking official was inspecting the sacks and writing figures in a scroll that was carried by a servant following him. Yoona guessed he had come all the way from Kaesong.

Yoona heard the farmers talking amongst themselves about the weather and other local news. She made her way past the farmers and sacks of rice and passed through an inner gate that led to another smaller courtyard. Groups of women squatted on straw mats and busied themselves peeling vegetables.

A dull thudding sound echoed in the courtyard as a man with a large wooden mallet pounded a slab of white dough. Yoona's mouth watered as she thought of the sweet rice cakes that would be made from the dough.

The voices of children carried over the walls. Yoona made her way to a side gate. She emerged into a large field outside the walls of the estate.

"Unni," called out Yoona's sister. Yuni had arrived earlier with her father and was with a group of children watching an archery contest.

Big Choi and the prince were standing at the edge of the field with bows and arrows. On the other side of the field was a series of targets.

The prince had already drawn his bow and aimed his arrow. He released the bow and the arrow shot forward. It soared in a gentle arc across the field and hit a target squarely in the middle with a *thunk*.

Big Choi nodded at this display of skill in archery. He notched an arrow in his bow and drew back the weapon. Big Choi focused his concentration on the target ahead of him. He let the arrow loose and it landed just off its mark. *Thunk*.

It was Mina's turn. Her bow was smaller and her target was set closer. She pulled an arrow from her quiver and notched it. Mina drew back the string and released the arrow. *Thunk.*

Yoona watched the contest and wished she could participate. Yoona had not grown up with the pursuits of the noble families such as archery and horseback riding.

"Would you like to try your hand at archery?" asked the prince as if he had read Yoona's mind.

"Oh no, no," said Yoona as she shook her head and tried to cover her face from embarrassment.

"Here, take the bow," said the prince as he offered his bow to Yoona. "Shooting a bow is just like writing hanja characters, it requires proper form and technique."

The prince seemed to be making amends for his previous dismissal of Yoona's writing skills. Yoona blushed as she recognized the weapon from the chest she had opened.

Yoona gripped the polished wood. The weapon felt strong and yet delicate in Yoona's hands. Yoona tried to pull back on the string. The bow resisted with an immense force.

"Hold the bow like this," said the prince.

The prince's arms were almost wrapped around Yoona as he guided her hands into the proper position. The prince notched an arrow into the bow for Yoona and gripped the bow with his left hand.

"Now pull back."

The prince was actually doing most of the work as Yoona pulled back the string and the bow bent into a curved position.

"Release the arrow."

The arrow flew across the field and landed on the target with a *thunk*. At that moment, Yoona felt a pang in her heart like an arrow had pierced it.

The rest of the afternoon passed by with various games and traditional harvest festival activities.

After the archery contest Yoona along with the rest of the children and the prince watched a wrestling match. Two stout men wearing only loincloths grappled with each other inside a dirt-floored ring. The crowd of farmers cheered and whooped while dignified noblemen watched the spectacle from beneath a shade tree.

A troupe of traveling acrobats demonstrated their skills in walking a tightrope and contorting themselves into odd positions. The farmers clapped and threw copper coins into a basket. Yoona wondered what far-flung corners of Korea these wandering performers had visited.

Groups of farmers with drums and gongs paraded through the fields, filling the valley with the clanging of their instruments. It was a joyous and exuberant sound and Yoona couldn't help feeling happy. The harvest was bountiful, the fall weather was mild and all was peaceful in the land.

Yoona heard the noblemen talking about foreign enemies and troubles in the northern frontier but it all seemed so far away.

The light darkened as afternoon turned into early evening. The sun settled into the horizon. Servants ran around Mina's estate lighting torches.

Yoona's eyes widened at the sight of watermelons being cut open. A wooden cutting table was rapidly getting soaked with juice as servants cut slice after slice with a carving knife. A crowd of little children gathered around.

Yoona waited and finally got a slice for herself. Just as she started to eat the watermelon, Yoona heard a wind-like roar and a collective gasp of wonder coming from outside the walls. The inky blackness of night glowed with a strange light.

Yoona rushed to the side gate and stepped outside.

A great bonfire was burning in a field. Yoona already felt its warmth against her face. The flames roared and sparkled and threw embers into the air. A crowd was gathering to observe the bonfire.

Yoona sat down on a bench underneath a small tree.

She watched as a servant tended the bonfire by adding more logs and poking at it with a stick.

Another person walked up and took a seat on the bench. It was the prince. He was holding a small bottle of rice wine.

"Good evening, Prince Lee."

The prince gave a polite nod to Yoona and took a drink from his bottle.

"The fire is rather magnificent, wouldn't you say?" said Yoona.

"It is." The prince paused. "It reminds me of when they burned down the palace."

Yoona looked at the prince with curiosity.

"For two hundred years the Lee Dynasty ruled the Kingdom of Dai Viet with a steady hand. Commerce, agriculture and learning flourished. We defeated foreign enemies at our borders and the kingdom was prosperous," said the prince.

"I understand you are a prince of the Lee family from Dai Viet?" said Yoona.

"Well, one of many. I am perhaps a third cousin of Prince Lee."

"But you are truly a prince?"

The prince laughed. "The ancestral lands of my father's family could fit inside this estate. We lived as humbly as farmers and worked the land with our own hands."

The prince shivered from the autumn cold. Yoona realized the prince had no suitable clothes for the coming cold season.

"I hear you come from a land where every season is like the summer," said Yoona.

"Yes, this changing of the seasons is quite new to me. What comes after this harvest season?"

"It gets very cold and dark and every plant and animal either dies or goes into a deep sleep. But after a while it gets warmer and warmer and everything is born again."

The prince took a drink from the bottle of rice wine and paused as if deep in thought.

"It is like the cycle of life. Birth and life and death and then rebirth. Perhaps it was meant to be. The Lee Dynasty was once strong and virtuous but had run its course."

"What happened?" asked Yoona.

"After two hundred years of peace, a long period of war followed. Rivals challenged the Lee Dynasty for the throne. In the end, we were defeated and lost everything."

"Everything?"

"I remember when what was left of the Lee clan fled in a small fleet of ships. Boats really, old and leaky things. My native land, getting smaller and smaller as the ocean swallowed us. It was the most crushing feeling, knowing you would never again see what you loved."

The bonfire crackled and roared as it burned brighter. Families gathered around the fire. Yoona saw young couples in the shadows laughing and holding hands.

The prince continued, "I was betrothed to a girl from another noble family. But after our great defeat I never heard from her or her family again."

"Oh no," said Yoona. She put her hand on the prince's hand to comfort him.

Yoona quickly pulled her hand back, feeling somewhat embarrassed. She folded her hands on her lap and turned her eyes downward. After a long pause Yoona spoke again, "But sometimes the end means the beginning of something new."

The bonfire flared up as pieces of burning wood collapsed. There was a sound of drums being beaten somewhere behind the walls.

Yoona realized her heart was beating furiously. She was so close to the prince. Yoona didn't know if the burning she felt on her cheeks was from the heat of the fire or something else. It seemed as though the prince was moving closer to Yoona . . .

"Ah ha! There they are!"

Big Choi was at the head of a procession of children. He pointed his fat finger at Yoona and the prince. The children were banging on gongs and little drums. Some of the boys wore hats with brightly-colored cloth streamers that waved in the air.

"Join us," Big Choi called out as he marched towards Yoona and the prince.

Big Choi took a drum from a child standing next to him and shoved it into the prince's hands. He turned over a small gong to Yoona. All at once Yoona found herself swept into the merry storm of noise-making children. She glanced around to find the prince but he too was swallowed up by the swirling crowd.

Chapter 11

After the harvest festival every household prepared for the coming winter. Farmers pickled and stored vegetables in clay jars that were sealed and buried in the ground.

The trees in the mountains shed all their leaves until only the pine trees remained green but the mild autumn weather seemed to hang on.

Yoona hoped the good weather would last longer but one morning she woke up and found herself shivering uncontrollably.

It's time to heat up the *ondol*, thought Yoona.

Every Korean house had an ondol heating system. The crawl space under the wood floors of a Korean house was made of masonry and built with flues. The flues carried the smoke from a source of fire such as the kitchen hearth.

The floors of the rooms above the flues would slowly heat up and radiate warmth to the rest of the room.

The ondol in Yoona's house was rather modest and heated up mostly the main room where Yoona's father studied and the guest room. A little bit of heat leaked into Yoona's bedroom and created a small spot of warmth in one corner of the floor. On cold winter nights Yoona huddled with her sister in this corner.

The ondol wasn't always kept burning hot but maintained in a smoldering state. Since it was the first cold day of winter, Yoona thought it was good to build a strong fire. The stones would get quite warm and stay like that for a while even after the fire died down.

Yoona blew on the embers of the hearth and soon had the fire burning steadily. She fed the fire with dried grass, waste material and wood. Warmth radiated from the previously cold hearth.

Yoona busied herself with boiling water for tea and cooking rice. She heard through the walls the sounds of everyone else in the house stirring.

The tea was finally done but the rice was still cooking. Yoona arranged the tea cups and pot on a tray and made her way to the main room. The prince and Yoona's father usually met early in the morning there. Yoona hoped the room would warm up soon.

Yoona slid open the doors. The room was empty. Yoona stepped inside with her bare feet. The floor wasn't cold but it wasn't quite yet warmed up.

Yoona arranged the tea cups on a small table. There was a sound of voices outside. The doors slid open and Yoona's father stepped in, followed by the prince.

"Good morning, appa. I hope you slept well," said Yoona.

"Good morning, my pretty one," replied Yoona's father.

The prince nodded silently at Yoona.

After the night of the harvest festival, the prince had maintained a polite and reserved manner with Yoona. He resumed his daily tutoring of her. Yoona in turn would explain an unfamiliar word or Korean custom to the prince from time to time.

Yoona found herself putting on her freshest hanbok and taking extra care with her appearance whenever she was scheduled to get tutored by the prince. Meanwhile, the prince always seemed as calm as the Enlightened One. Yoona often wondered what was on his mind.

Yoona kneeled and arranged the tea set on the table. As it was the custom in those days, Yoona's father and the prince were seated on the floor. While a Korean room might have a chest or two and a writing table, upright chairs were not part of the décor.

The tea set up was done. Yoona felt the floor getting warm beneath her bare feet. She bowed to the two men and exited the room.

Yoona was back in the kitchen. The fire in the hearth was now burning hot. Yoona tossed into the flames a couple more pieces of scrap wood and dried grass. The flames surged with a brief roar.

Yoona turned her attention to the food. She washed out a small iron pot and poured rice and water into it. Yoona opened up a clay jar of pickled vegetables. A bit of dried fish provided some flavor.

Yoona waited for the rice to finish cooking. The hearth was getting quite cozy and warm and Yoona didn't want to leave it. Finally, the rice was done. What used to be hard little grains was now soft and chewy and quite delicious.

The iron pot of rice breathed out puffs of steam. Yoona and her sister usually had to eat coarser grains such as barley, so Yoona could only feast with her senses of smell and sight on the white rice.

The white rice reminded Yoona of the pile of goose down she had been collecting the past year. Wild geese visited a nearby pond and Yoona would collect the soft down the geese molted and clean it. Yoona wanted to make a new winter blanket for herself and Yuni but she decided to make something else.

Yoona set the food on a tray and went back to the meeting room. She set her bare feet on the floor and found it quite warm. Yoona started arranging the food on the table.

"I had the strangest dream this morning," said the prince to Yoona's father.

Yoona's father nodded silently.

The prince continued, "I dreamt I was a chicken getting boiled over a fire. The flames kept on getting hotter and hotter."

Yoona stole a glance at the prince.

The prince was sitting on the floor with his hands folded on his lap. His back was as straight as a board. The prince cast his eyes at the table to show respect for Yoona's father. The prince had a calm expression but he looked as though he was struggling to maintain it. Little beads of sweat formed on the prince's forehead.

"Are there any volcanoes in Korea?" the prince asked Yoona's father.

"Volcanoes?"

"There's a story in my native country of a fierce dragon that was terrorizing the land. Finally a brave warrior captured the dragon and buried it. Soon, smoke and heat came out of the earth. The flat ground started swelling until it became a mountain. The dragon remains trapped inside the mountain to this day."

"Yoona, do we have any volcanoes in Korea?"

"Baekdusan, appa."

"Ah yes. The White Mountain," said Yoona's father. "The Korean people originally came from this mountain in the north. The earth around this mountain boils and steams like something not of this world, I hear."

"How far is this Baekdusan from here?"

Yoona's father stroked his beard and looked up at the ceiling. "Not too far, perhaps a journey of several days."

The floor of the room was getting warmer and warmer. A single bead of sweat rolled down the prince's face.

Yoona's father had already started his meal. The rice was still warm and little clouds of steam rose up as Yoona's father dug into it with his chopsticks.

Yoona in the meantime tidied up the room. She folded up a futon and put it back into a wooden chest. Yoona was enjoying the cozy warmth of the room and didn't want to go back outside.

"Ahhhhh!" the prince cried suddenly as he jumped up from his seat. Both Yoona and her father stopped their activities and looked at the prince. His face was deep red.

"We must leave this area immediately! A volcano is going to erupt beneath this house," said the prince.

Yoona's father looked startled for a moment. He then smiled.

"Yoona, please show our guest the ondol system we use to keep ourselves warm," said Yoona's father.

Yoona and the prince went outside together. Yoona made her way to the hearth, with the prince following. She showed the prince the roaring fire inside.

Yoona and the prince then walked around and outside the house. Yoona showed the prince a chimney from which the smoke finally escaped.

The prince nodded, his curiosity finally satisfied. Yoona and the prince exited the kitchen and walked together in silence until the prince spoke up.

"I want to apologize for my sudden outburst earlier. I was so surprised at the way the floor was heating up. I have never encountered such a thing before."

"Oh, that's quite okay. We Koreans are used to the ondol, it keeps us warm in the winter," Yoona replied.

Yoona glanced at the prince. The prince had assumed his usual stoic demeanor. His face was darkened from his work in the fields during the harvest. The prince's unruly hair had grown out some and was now tied up in the Korean way. Only his eyes seemed to hint at the unknown emotions that lurked beneath the surface.

"My prince, you know it's not such a bad thing to show one's feelings," said Yoona to the prince as the two stepped back into the warm main room.

Chapter 12

A Korean winter can be quite harsh. The bone-chilling winds blow straight down from the north and swirl through the valleys and around the mountains.

The winter season was when everyone in the village huddled indoors. The farmers repaired their tools while the women mended clothes or spun new thread. Scholars such as Yoona's father buried themselves deeper inside their books.

As for Yoona, she was busy with the goose down she had collected over the past year. A straw basket in one corner of Yoona's room was overflowing with the white feathers.

Yoona had already sewn an insulated vest for her sister that was made up of numerous quilt-like sealed air pockets holding the goose down inside. Yoona was now making another one just like her sister's but larger.

Yoona stayed up late one evening putting the finishing touches on the quilted vest. It was finally finished. Yoona carefully folded up the vest and made her way to the prince's quarters.

The prince was in the main room playing a game of *baduk* with Yoona's father. Baduk was a board game from China that involved black and white pieces played against each other, moving around to capture territory. It was a game of strategic maneuvering and war.

Yoona placed the vest in a corner of the prince's room where she often dropped off clean laundry.

Yoona woke up the next morning and found the world buried under fresh snowfall, the first of the season. The roof of the house was covered in snow and the courtyard was piled high with snow drifts.

At first Yoona was happy at the sight of the winter wonderland. She had many memories of playing in the snow as a small child.

Yoona then thought of having to clear the snow from the steps of the house with a broom. She thought of having to dig through the snow and frozen ground for a buried root to cook and eat.

Yoona sighed. Growing up meant more responsibilities and less fun.

Yoona was in the kitchen warming up the hearth when she heard laughter outside, a joyous sound. Curious, Yoona looked out into the courtyard.

The prince and Yuni were both playing in the fresh snow. The prince was lying down in a snow drift, waving his arms and legs. Meanwhile Yuni was grabbing handfuls of snow and throwing it into the air, creating a small snowstorm above the prince's head.

Yoona saw the prince was wearing the quilted vest she had sewn for him.

The prince noticed Yoona's presence. He immediately got up and dusted the snow off his clothes.

"Oh, I didn't see you there . . . I got a little carried away. I've never seen snow in my life. What I meant to say is . . . I have seen it in my native land. High up in the mountains but I never got close enough to touch it."

The prince's face was starting to flush.

"Did you make this vest for me? It is quite warm," continued the prince.

Yoona nodded.

"Well, I should be going back in," said the prince.

Yoona scooped up a handful of snow as the prince turned around. Yoona's hands were small so the snowball she made was quite tiny. Yoona threw the snowball at the prince.

"Hey!" said the prince as the snowball hit him.

As the prince turned around, another tiny snowball hit him, this time coming from Yuni. The prince hastily scooped up some snow and threw it at Yoona. Soon, the three of them were laughing and playing in the snow.

Despite the cold weather, Yoona felt a growing warmth inside of her. She was seeing for the first time the prince in an unguarded and joyful mood. Yoona wondered if this cold winter would turn out to be the warmest season after all.

Chapter 13

The cold winds continued to blow down the mountains and through the valleys after the first snow. After a couple more snowfalls the land was under winter's icy grip.

Big Choi had heard of the prince's skill at baduk and came over once a week to play the prince. Big Choi often found himself beating the prince. He finally found a pursuit he was better at than the prince.

One day Big Choi had come over by himself and was playing a round with the prince.

Yoona was in the room with her sister, working on some sewing. Their father was in the next room taking a nap.

"I hear the northern barbarians have retreated for the winter," said Big Choi. "But in the springtime they will resume their war."

"How serious of a threat are these foreign invaders to the kingdom?" asked the prince.

"The barbarians have already seized the northern provinces of China. They are constantly attacking our northern defenses and taking territory. The Korean king may have to raise a large army when the weather gets warmer to battle them."

The prince looked at the sword and dagger Big Choi had brought along with him.

"You are well armed, perhaps in preparation for future battle with these barbarians?" asked the prince.

"Oh, those? One must be careful when traveling now. There's a tiger prowling the hills these days."

Yoona and Yuni stopped their sewing and looked at Big Choi.

Big Choi laughed. "You haven't heard? No one has seen the beast yet in person, but the villagers found tracks in the snow. Big tracks."

In those days, tigers lived not only in India but in the northern steppes and were quite common in the forested mountains of Korea. A tiger is normally an elusive beast and prefers to avoid humans. But given the right circumstances the tiger can be a very dangerous creature.

"I'm sure it is just passing through for the winter," said

Big Choi.

The room was warm from the ondol but Yoona shivered at the thought of the tiger in the mountains.

Chapter 14

The winter days and nights passed by seemingly without end.

Yoona mended more clothes, spun thread and practiced her calligraphy. She wondered at times if there really was a big tiger in the mountains nearby. Yoona felt safe within the walls of the house. All of the food from the harvest was stored inside and the chickens were safe in their coops. There was no need to go outside of the house walls for now.

Occasionally, Yoona would hear about a farmer who lost a pig or another who woke up one morning and found his chicken coop destroyed. But such things happened all the time. It was a fact of life that wolves, bears and even tigers lived in the surrounding forests and mountains.

One clear winter day Mina and her mother paid a visit to Yoona's house. Accompanying them were three male servants from their household, armed with heavy wooden clubs.

Yoona and Mina sat together in Yoona's room.

"Mina, I noticed you came with a group of men. And they were carrying weapons," said Yoona.

"Yes, for extra safety."

"Safety?"

"Remember that story about a tiger in the mountains? My father said it might be a man-eater."

"A man-eater?" Yoona asked.

"Well, since he's the governor of the province he received news of such a beast earlier this season in another village, about a day's journey from here. A farmer was attacked in the fields and . . . killed."

Yoona gasped.

"My father summoned a tiger hunter from another province after that incident. The hunter is going to make it up here soon. In the meantime, everyone has been instructed to stay inside and go out only in large groups," said Mina.

Back in those days there existed a tough breed of men called tiger hunters in Korea. These men made a living tracking and killing tigers that became too troublesome. They often lived a life that was as solitary and wandering as that of their prey, traveling from province to province wherever their services were needed.

Yoona wondered what sort of fearsome beast a man-eating tiger was. She wondered what sort of person a tiger hunter was.

Chapter 15

One day the tiger hunter arrived in the village. Yoona didn't see him herself. She heard about his arrival from the farmer who tilled the land for Yoona's father.

The farmer was in the courtyard talking to Yoona's father. Yoona peeked through a hole in a door at the two men.

"Teacher, I saw him with my own eyes as he was walking down the village street. Everyone was so frightened of him. His eyes were yellow like a tiger's and he carried a crossbow," said the farmer.

"Did anyone welcome him to our village?"

"No one dared leave their houses. Just the sight of his face made a child cry. We all just watched him from behind closed doors. Where he was going, no one knew."

"I imagine he's headed to the governor's place. Tiger hunters must be paid, after all."

"Teacher, how long do you think he will be here for? Everyone is so frightened of him."

"There are dangerous beasts in this world and brave men must fight them. I remember in my youth a hunter who was hired to hunt a tiger that terrorized the entire province. It took the hunter most of the season to track and kill the animal," said Yoona's father.

"Well, as soon as both the tiger and the hunter leave this valley, the better," said the farmer.

That night Yoona tossed and turned in bed and had a frightening dream. She was running through the woods. Something was behind her, chasing her, something fierce and dangerous. Yoona could feel its breath on her back.

Suddenly, Yoona tripped and started falling down a hill and came to a stop at the bottom of a tree.

Except it wasn't a tree.

A gigantic man towered over Yoona. He was dressed in animal skins and armed with a crossbow. He had a wild beard. The man's eyes were yellow and seemed to burn like coals and his face was browned like a roasted chestnut.

And his teeth! The man snarled and bared his teeth that

looked like long knives . . .

Yoona woke up, her heart beating wildly.

"Unni?" said Yuni. Yuni was right beside Yoona in bed and looking at her with eyes that were still groggy with sleep.

"Oh Yuni! What a frightening dream I had," said Yoona. She held her little sister tight in her arms.

Yoona remembered what her father said about dangerous things in the world. She thought about how when she was her sister's age the world seemed to be a different place. It was a place with shadows, for sure. But for the most part Yoona's childhood world was a happy and sunlit place.

Yoona remembered back then her mother was still alive. She wanted to cry into her pillow at this thought but she remembered Yuni was at her side. Yoona sniffled a little, wiped her nose and went back to sleep.

Yoona didn't mind too much being confined mostly to her house. It was winter and the rest of the village was staying indoors too.

The farmers walked outside only in groups of three or more individuals, armed with wooden clubs. Women and children were rarely seen outside their homes. Yoona sometimes dashed to the grove of trees just outside the house walls to collect firewood.

One morning Yoona stepped outside and saw paw prints in the fresh snow. She ran back inside, her heart pounding. Yoona remembered the night before she had heard strange noises beyond the walls, a rustling of bushes followed by a low growling.

Yoona felt too scared to go outside again that morning. She convinced her father in the afternoon to examine the paw prints. However, the morning snowfall was just a light dusting of flakes and the paw prints were gone, blown away by the winds.

Yoona thought the hunter was as elusive as the tiger.

The hunter slept in the woods and spent his days tracking the animal. Some of the villagers thought the tiger wasn't even in the valley anymore and had wandered hundreds of miles away by now. Then a farmer would wake up and find a sheep missing.

Sometimes Yoona looked off into the distant hills and saw a wisp of smoke rising up from the treetops. She wondered what it would be like to sleep in the woods with only the night sky over one's head.

A couple weeks passed. The shortest day of the year had come and gone and the daylight hours were getting longer. Yoona wondered if the tiger would move on when the season got warmer and the food more abundant.

One day the farmer dropped by Yoona's house with great news.

"Teacher, the hunter got the tiger!" the farmer said to Yoona's father. Yoona looked through the open gate and saw children running towards the main street of the village. The farmer rushed off after delivering the news.

"Appa, let's go," Yoona said to her father, who was rendering ink strokes on paper.

"Would the proper hanja character be 'knowledge' or 'wisdom' in this passage, I wonder?" said Yoona's father to himself.

"Appa!" said Yoona.

"You can go by yourself. I'll stay here with Yuni. I'm not sure she's old enough to see such things."

"Oh, appa!" said Yoona as she left the room. She snatched a fur cap to keep herself warm and ran outside.

The cold air hit Yoona's cheeks with a sharp slap as she ran down the dirt path. Winter had not loosened its grip on the land.

A large crowd was huddled together in the distance. Yoona ran past fields that were just patches of ice and bare earth. She ran down a steep path and past farmhouses.

Yoona felt good to be free from the confines of the

house. She was happy with the realization that the frozen earth would soon start giving life to flowers and crops again. Yoona thought it was good to not live in fear of unknown dangers.

Yoona finally got closer to the crowd. She felt overwhelmed by all the people gathered around. Excited chatter rose into the air. Yoona tried to stand on her toes but she could barely look over the shoulders of the people in front of her.

The crowd shifted and Yoona got a glimpse of what everyone was pointing at and whispering about.

It was just the briefest look, a flash of black and orange stripes and tufts of white fur and a glimpse of a man with a black beard and fierce-looking eyes. The crowd shifted again and Yoona found herself staring at a wall of people.

"The governor is here," someone in the crowd shouted. Mina's father appeared on horseback. He was followed by a group of servants.

Mina's father was dressed in fine robes and carried a sword by his side. He seemed to wear the sword awkwardly. Although he was the governor and a great landowner, Mina's father was at heart a scholar like Yoona's father.

All of the villagers and the tiger hunter kneeled and bowed their heads before Mina's father in respect.

Mina's father dismounted from his horse and faced the crowd. "Today is a new day. Peace has returned to our valley," said Mina's father. The crowd gave a murmur of approval.

Mina's father said something to one of his servants and soon the dead tiger was trussed up on a pole and carried away.

One of the villagers who was a medicine man was already talking to Mina's father about taking the tiger's gallbladder for his use. The crowd began to disperse, discussing the upcoming planting season and the weather.

Yoona looked again at the tiger hunter.

The tiger hunter wasn't a giant like Yoona had imagined him to be. In fact the hunter was small and lean like a house cat. His face was weathered from a life of living outdoors. Yoona wondered if the hunter would open his mouth and reveal his teeth but he appeared to be a man of few words.

The hunter slung his pack and weapons over his shoulder and started walking towards the distant mountains. His job was done.

Yoona watched the hunter get smaller and smaller, until he finally disappeared into the mountains. Yoona wondered what part of Korea the tiger hunter was headed.

Life was back to normal for now.

Chapter 16

A couple weeks passed. The days were getting warmer but the day-to-day weather was fickle. A freezing but snowless day might be followed by rain showers the next.

One day the season finally brought temperatures that weren't too chilly, with clear skies.

Yoona decided to take advantage of the mild weather to go digging in the hills for rare roots. Her father had taken ill with a slight cold and Yoona thought it was best to cook him a soothing broth.

Yoona equipped herself with a stick for digging and a basket. She ran into the prince while leaving the house.

"Good morning, Prince Lee," said Yoona.

The prince was saddling up his horse. A bow and quiver of arrows was slung over his shoulders. The prince had contributed much to the household during the winter with his hunting, bringing in rabbits and other game.

"Good morning, my princess," said the prince with a courtly bow.

The prince was just being lighthearted but Yoona felt her cheeks flush. She hurried away.

Yoona was soon climbing the hills behind the village. The area was thick with pine trees and bushes that remained green even in winter.

Yoona started to dig around for medicinal roots among the undergrowth. The prince was further down in the valley. He had dismounted from his horse and was looking for small game.

After Yoona had been digging for a while her basket was half-filled with roots and plants. It was enough to make a hearty soup for Yoona's father.

Yoona was making her way down a hill when she saw something that made her stop dead in her tracks. At the bottom of the hill was a creek and drinking from this creek was a tiger.

Yoona immediately recognized the black and orange markings of the animal. Her heart was pounding. Yoona slowly backed up the hill. The tiger hadn't seen her yet.

Crack!

Yoona bit her lip as she stepped on a twig. She tried to think quickly. Yoona remembered there was another path that went over and around the hill and back to the village.

Yoona picked up a stone that was lying on the ground. What use is a stone against a fierce beast, thought Yoona. She felt like crying as she tossed the stone away. Yoona looked around for the prince but he was gone.

Yoona was now on the path back to the village.

The tiger was out of sight. Yoona walked with slow but steady steps. She quickened her pace. The surrounding woods felt strangely empty. The bare branches of the trees looked like the claws of an animal. Not even a bird was chirping. The only sound was the *swish swish* of Yoona's clothes as she hurried along the path.

Yoona gripped her basket tightly. She resolved to run as fast as she could as soon as there was some distance between her and the tiger.

The path became narrow and winding. Scrubby bushes grew on both sides. Thorns and sharp branches scratched at Yoona's face.

Yoona thought she heard noises in the woods, as if some large animal was moving fast through the undergrowth. There was a sound of breaking branches and rustling leaves.

Yoona dropped the basket and dashed through the

woods as fast as she could. Suddenly, there was a flash of orange and black fur and a deafening roar. Yoona screamed.

Everything went dark as Yoona closed her eyes. She felt the sensation of being lifted up from the ground.

"Hold on as tight as you can," said a firm voice. Yoona felt as if she was riding a horse. She felt the up and down motion of the animal as it galloped through the woods.

Yoona had her arms wrapped around the torso of the horse rider, as if she was hugging a tree. Her eyes were still tightly shut.

The horse was moving fast, as if something was chasing it. Tree branches snapped and whipped Yoona as they passed by.

Yoona heard the familiar *thwack* of a bow string. The horse rider had shot a bow and arrow. The horse rider cursed to himself. He had missed whatever he was trying to hit.

Yoona felt as though she was being thrown around and over a rugged landscape of steep hills and craggy rocks.

Thwack went another arrow.

There was an angry roar followed by the sound of a heavy body falling on rocks.

The horse stumbled and came to a standstill. Silence

followed.

"Yoona, everything is okay now."

Yoona opened her eyes. She was sitting backwards on the horse, face to face with the prince. Yoona realized she was holding on to the prince with all her might. She loosened her grip and the two dismounted from the horse.

Yoona found herself looking down a steep cliff. Bright red splotches marked the rock face.

The prince was examining his horse. The hide of the animal was covered with numerous scratches. A deep series of gashes revealed a fierce animal had clawed the horse.

"There must have been two tigers in the area, perhaps a male and female," said the prince.

The prince's face had many small cuts and his clothing was torn in places.

"Prince Lee, we need to get this patched up," said Yoona as she tried to tie up a piece of the prince's shirt that was hanging loose.

Yoona wasn't sure whether she or the prince had drawn closer first but suddenly, all at once, Yoona found herself in the prince's arms.

"Oh, Prince Lee," Yoona cried softly.

Yoona felt her heart pounding fiercely. She wished she

could be in the prince's arms for as long as possible. The prince gave Yoona a gentle kiss on her forehead and the two were once again separated.

"Shall we head back?" asked the prince. The prince lifted up Yoona and put her on his horse, facing the right way this time. The prince mounted the horse so that he was behind Yoona.

It had been a long day, thought Yoona as she and the prince made their way back home.

Chapter 17

A couple weeks had passed since Yoona's encounter with the tiger. Today the weather was warm enough for Yoona's father to sit outside on the veranda and play a game of baduk with Mina's father.

The prince was playing his own game of baduk with Big Choi. Yoona had claimed a portion of the veranda for herself and used it to put out various herbs and roots to dry.

The talk among the older men soon turned to the war that was brewing at the northern frontier.

Whenever enemies from the north attacked, springtime was when the fighting resumed. The northerners spent the winter stockpiling food and repairing weapons. As the weather got warmer the grasses in the fields grew and allowed the northerners to feed their war horses.

"I heard the northern barbarians defeated a Korean army at the border. They are now planning an attack on our capital city," said Mina's father. He moved a black piece on the baduk board.

Yoona's father looked at the board and pondered his next move.

"We need to outmaneuver them, crush their armies," said Big Choi as he waved his hands around excitedly. Big Choi had no experience with real war. He was beating the prince easily in baduk though.

"I have already sent Mina and her mother to Hanyang, further south," said Mina's father to Yoona's father.

Seoul was known as Hanyang in those days.

"My servants will leave behind a mule with supplies, if you wish to leave for Hanyang with your daughters. Although I do think our valley will be safe from the barbarians," continued Mina's father.

"Almost every invasion force in the past five hundred years has passed through this valley," said Big Choi with an air of authority. He moved another piece on the baduk board. Yoona didn't know the rules of baduk but it looked as though the prince's pieces were surrounded.

"The king has asked every governor to help raise an army," said Mina's father. "Many of the eldest sons of the noble families in the valley have already taken up arms."

The prince turned around and faced Mina's father and bowed deeply.

"Teacher, I wish to be at your service. I have fought many battles in my native land and wish to defend my new home," said the prince.

"Excellent! The Korean king is assembling an army at Kaesong. The volunteers from the valley will be leaving for the capital in a few days," said Mina's father.

Big Choi in the meantime was silently brooding over the baduk board. Yoona wondered what was going on in his mind.

Soon, the first day of spring arrived. The flowering trees in the valley were exploding with pale pink and white blossoms.

It seemed as though the entire population of the valley was gathered around the front gate of Mina's family estate. Old and young, farmers and noble families, everyone was present.

Lined up before the front gate was a small group of young men on horses, armed with swords, lances and bows. Many of the noble sons were wearing fine suits of armor that were last used by their fathers in a long ago war. Others only had a helmet and thick leather vest to protect them. Their horses carried packs of supplies to last several days.

Yoona's heart leapt as she recognized the prince among the group. He was wearing his dented battle helmet, the same one Yoona had seen before in his room. The prince's sword was at his side and his bow was slung over his shoulder.

Yoona wanted to rush up to the prince and give him a farewell embrace but it would have been too embarrassing with the crowd of people present.

"The governor is coming," a shout went up among the crowd.

The doors of the main gate opened with a creaking of heavy wood. Mina's father stepped out. He was dressed in the fine robes and hat of his office. Everyone bowed before him.

"A little while ago our peaceful valley was terrorized by a fierce tiger, or rather two fierce tigers," said Mina's father. Yoona glanced at the prince and caught him glancing at her.

Mina's father continued, "The world is full of tigers and brave young men such as these must go and fight them. May the heavens watch over them and bring them safely back to us."

A murmur went through the gathered crowd.

A monk from the local temple was present. He walked up to each young man and blessed him and his weapons.

A crying mother went to her son and handed him a sack of rice. Soon other villagers approached the young men and handed them coins and food. Little children tossed flowers. Yoona took the opportunity to rush up to the prince.

The prince was sitting high on his horse. Yoona grabbed the prince's hand and held it to her cheek.

"Oh! Prince Lee, please promise me you'll come back safely," cried Yoona.

The prince squeezed Yoona's hand tightly in response. The two were soon separated as the crowd pushed in from all sides. Eventually everyone made their final farewells. Small firecrackers went off with a popping sound and the young men rode off into the distant hills.

Chapter 18

The weather was getting warmer and the days longer. Once again, the laughter of children playing outdoors became a familiar sound.

The early spring bloom of trees faded and fell away, leaving the ground beneath them blanketed with a snow-like covering of flower petals. The farmers talked about the spring planting and the livestock giving birth.

It was a joyous time of rebirth but Yoona felt an aching loneliness in her heart. She would sometimes pause in the middle of a task such as carrying water and think about the prince.

Where could he be right now? Was he marching through some desolate valley in the north? Was the prince fighting in a fierce battle with the enemy? Yoona tried hard not to dwell on that last thought.

Once, Yoona overheard the farmers talking about the war in the north. An old man jabbered about a village in another valley that was overrun and all of its inhabitants slaughtered. It all seemed so far away though. The hills and mountains that stretched into the distance seemed as peaceful as ever.

The springtime brought forth an abundance of useful roots and berries.

One day Yoona was alone in the hills foraging for plants. Yoona missed the company of Mina and wondered what she was doing these days.

Today Yoona had ventured a little further than she usually did. She walked over a hill and looked over the valley below.

The valley was narrow and surrounded by steep mountains that served as a wall around it. An opening between the mountains controlled access to the valley from the outside world. A tall stone wall and massive gate ran across this opening.

Close to the wall an estate was in the process of being renovated and expanded. Numerous workers swarmed around the place. Stone masons chiseled away at blocks of stone and carpenters climbed over half-finished buildings.

It was Big Choi's family estate.

Yoona made her way down the hill that overlooked the estate and spotted Big Choi. He was leading a group of boys, some of them younger than Yoona. They were armed with bamboo sticks sharpened at the ends.

"Good afternoon, Yoona," said Big Choi. He turned around and gave orders to a man who appeared to be twice his age.

Big Choi turned his attention back to Yoona. "My father has left for Kaesong to advise the king on the matter with the northern barbarians and left me in charge. He's had extensive dealings with these barbarians and can even speak their language. I've learned a little myself, too."

"It looks like the construction on your family estate is moving along," said Yoona. The buildings seemed to be built stronger than those on Mina's estate. The walls were higher and the foundations thicker.

"My father was able to convince the king it was of strategic importance to strengthen the valley's defenses," said Big Choi as he pointed north at the gate and walls that stretched across the opening between two mountains.

"Whoever controls that passage controls access to the valley. Whoever controls the valley controls the entire region," said Big Choi.

"Follow me, I'll show you something," Big Choi continued.

Big Choi dismissed the other boys. The boys dropped their weapons and ran off to play games. Yoona walked with Big Choi down a path that led to the surrounding hills. The two were soon hiking up a steep slope.

Large mounds of earth that were cleared of trees and planted with grass appeared. It was the ancestral burial grounds of Big Choi's family. Yoona and Big Choi pressed on further. Smaller mounds appeared. These were untended, with tall grass growing on them.

"Do you know how old these tombs are?" said Big Choi, pointing to the overgrown grass mounds in front of Yoona.

Yoona shook her head.

"These tombs are hundreds and hundreds of years old. The oldest tombs are not ours but belonged to a local ruler my family defeated long ago," said Big Choi.

"Look over the valley, near those cliffs," Big Choi continued.

Yoona spotted what appeared to be the ruins of an ancient wall.

"Time passes, kingdoms come and go. Great families are ruined, others rise in their place. Even the Korean king . . ."

Big Choi paused mid-sentence. It was considered a great offense to say anything inauspicious about the Korean royal family. He stomped on an insect that crossed his path.

"I believe our family is on the rise and we will once again be great," continued Big Choi. After making that remark, he grabbed Yoona.

"Big Choi, please," Yoona cried out as she pulled away.

Big Choi loosened his grip on Yoona and laughed. "Is that foreign prince still on your mind, Yoona? His people lost a struggle for power in their native land and came here with nothing."

"He is brave and fighting our enemies," said Yoona.

"He is foolish and will most likely perish. The northern barbarians are fierce and strong. They spend their entire adult lives in a constant state of war and have wiped out entire armies sent to fight them."

Yoona shuddered.

She wondered if what Big Choi was saying was true. Yoona was now walking with him among the ruined walls. Nearby was what appeared to be the remains of a foundation for a house. Old broken stones were scattered on the ground and wild grasses grew everywhere.

Yoona felt overwhelmed by the fleeting nature of everything in the world: the scent of the spring blooms, the gentle breeze that blew through her hair, the crumbling walls of the house that once stood in the field. Everything had come and gone.

"Well . . . if the prince survives . . . I think he will . . . surely he'll return to the valley . . ." said Yoona. She was struggling to hold back her emotions.

Big Choi laughed. "If he returns. Hope for an unknown future is foolish. The only thing that matters is the present."

Big Choi's family estate was now in view. It took up as much land as a small village, with many storehouses and buildings under construction.

"Yoona, think about what I said," said Big Choi as he and Yoona reached a fork in the path. It was time for the two to go their separate ways. Big Choi had always been a round and well-fed child, hence his nickname. Today his face looked hard and cruel.

After a long hike through the hills, Yoona was back home. The place looked rather small compared to Big Choi's sprawling estate. A single storehouse on Big Choi's estate was bigger than Yoona's home.

"Appa!" cried Yoona as she rushed into her father's study room. Yoona's father was hunched over his writing desk. Yoona hugged her father.

"What's the matter, my pretty daughter?"

"Appa, I'm so afraid."

"Of what? There are no tigers in the mountains now."

"I don't know. It feels like the world is full of tigers."

"It's okay, you're safe here," said Yoona's father.

Just then a strong gust of wind blew and rattled the wood-framed paper doors of the room. Yoona closed her eyes and hoped her father was right as she hugged him tighter.

Chapter 19

A couple days later the first one showed up, tired and hungry.

The soldier's armor was punctured in places and his clothes ragged. A crowd of curious villagers gathered around him as the soldier trudged into the village. The soldier's sword dragged behind him like a useless and broken tool. The soldier begged the villagers for food and water.

One of the villagers gave the soldier a rice ball, another a small piece of meat. Yoona had just visited the well and gave the soldier a cup of water. The man took everything with his rough hands and stuffed it into his mouth. After he was satisfied, it was the villagers' turn to satisfy their hunger for news about the outside world.

"In a battle north of here, the enemy defeated a Korean army. The barbarians chased down the remaining soldiers with their horses and shot them down with arrows. A few of us managed to escape into the hills," the soldier said as he sat underneath a shade tree.

The villagers gathered around the soldier shook their heads and murmured *aigoo aigoo.*

Yoona felt quite anxious. She wanted to ask the soldier if the prince was in the battle. Yoona realized it was futile. One might as well ask the man which one was which among all the birds flying in the skies.

The soldier sat underneath the tree for most of the afternoon. Some of the villagers wandered away while others stood over him like bees hovering around a flower and peppered the soldier with questions. The evening came and one of the villagers offered the soldier a place to rest for the night.

The next day a couple of other soldiers wandered into the village. Two of the soldiers carried on their shoulders a third one who couldn't walk because of an injury.

As the day went on, groups of two or three soldiers showed up in a slow trickle. They were all tired and beaten and their weapons broken or lost.

The villagers tended them as best as they could. Mina's

father provided the soldiers with sleeping quarters and food on his estate. By the end of the day, it seemed a small army or at least what remained of an army was camped out in the village.

The next day Yoona was in the hills when she heard what sounded like thunder. It came from the north and seemed to roll down the valley. Yoona rushed down to the village and hid among some bushes.

The rumbling sound grew louder.

A horde of warriors mounted on horses burst into the village. The warriors resembled the tiger hunter, with dark weathered faces and fierce eyes.

A group of Korean soldiers came out of a farmer's house to fight the newcomers. One of the mounted enemy warriors pulled out his bow and notched an arrow in the weapon.

Thunk! One of the Korean soldiers crumpled to the ground. *Thunk!* Another soldier fell with an arrow in his chest. *Thunk!* The last soldier was dispatched as though he was a rabbit being hunted.

The warrior on horseback charged into the farmer's house. A screaming farmer and his family ran out. Moments later the warrior charged back out.

A wisp of smoke floated out of the doorway. Soon,

flames were shooting through the roof as the paper, wood and straw of the house caught fire.

The enemy warriors thundered back and forth through the village on their horses. Hazy smoke and the smell of burnt wood drifted through the streets as other farmhouses were set on fire. The crying of children and the wailing of women pierced the air.

Eventually the sounds of battle died down. The Korean soldiers were all dead or dying. The warriors on horseback herded the villagers as if they were cattle. The villagers were being pushed towards an open space.

Yoona crawled through the underbrush and hid herself behind a wall. The smoke from the fires and crying of little children and animals provided good cover.

One of the warriors appeared to be the leader. He rode a large black horse and wore a fearsome-looking battle helmet that made him look like a bird of prey.

The warrior on horseback dragged a Korean man behind him. The man was bound with ropes and struggled to keep up with the mounted warrior. Sometimes he stumbled and the warrior gave the rope a sharp tug.

The man on the ground was Mina's father.

Chapter 20

The governor's clothing was torn and hanging in places and his face was bruised and bloodied, as if he had received a thorough beating. Yoona almost cried out when she saw Mina's father in such a state.

Mina's father tried to maintain a dignified air as he stumbled and walked through the mud of the village streets. He finally collapsed into a heap.

The barbarian warriors were gathered around Mina's father. All of the villagers were on their knees with their faces touching the ground. Low moans and sobs rose up from time to time among the villagers.

Yoona imagined one of the warriors spotted her and ducked down behind the wall. She heard a familiar voice addressing the crowd.

"Today is a tragic day. A mighty storm has come from the north. The weak must make way for the strong."

Yoona looked through a small opening in the wall. The speaker was Big Choi. He paused as the barbarian leader standing next to him spoke to him in a foreign tongue. Big Choi nodded in response.

Big Choi continued, "Farmers, go back to your fields. The northerners will not hurt you if you respect them."

A moan came from a mortally-wounded villager who was lying in a ditch. One by one the villagers crawled and limped back to their homes. The smell of charred wood lingered in the air.

A stray pig squealed and ran through the village. One of the barbarians drew his bow and let loose an arrow. The pig let out one final squeal, ran around in circles and collapsed on the ground.

Yoona wanted to cry.

Yoona rushed home and found her father comforting Yuni. She ran into her father's arms.

"Oh appa, what's happening to the world?" Yoona asked.

"I don't know, I wish I knew," said Yoona's father as he held his two daughters close.

Chapter 21

The full spring season came to the hills in a glory of blossoming greenery and life in the valley for the most part did return to normal.

The farmers repaired their houses and went back to their planting. The barbarians would seize a pig or chicken from a farmer every so often but they seemed to have no taste for the rice and other grains stored over the winter.

The barbarians set up their camp in the vast courtyards of Mina's family estate. They rode their horses carelessly through the place and punched holes in the walls of the buildings for sport.

As for Mina's father, the old governor was rumored to be confined to one room in his estate, watched over by a guard.

One day Yoona was searching the hills for berries. She had traveled further than usual and was about to make her way down a path that led out of the valley.

"Halt!" A voice called out.

A boy younger than Yoona blocked the path. He held a sharpened bamboo stick in his hand. Yoona recognized him as one of the boys who always followed around Big Choi.

"No one is to leave the valley without permission," said the boy.

"Sangho-*ya*, who gives such orders? Have we not always wandered these hills without care?" asked Yoona as she offered the boy some of the berries she had already picked.

The boy's demeanor softened as he took the berries.

"Big Choi told us there was a new power in the kingdom and . . . and . . ." said the boy. He looked at the ground and lowered the stick.

The boy's face became hard again. "How dare you address me with such disrespect. No one leaves this valley without permission. Especially you, Yoona."

The boy pointed his bamboo stick at Yoona menacingly.

"Okay, I understand," said Yoona as she bowed to the

boy and turned around.

The next day Yoona was at home with her father and Yuni when Big Choi showed up. He was wearing his sword and was accompanied by several boys armed with bamboo sticks.

Big Choi greeted Yoona's father with traditional deference but the gesture seemed hollow, as if Big Choi was doing it only for appearances.

"Household inspection, mandated for all families in the valley," said Big Choi.

The boys with bamboo sticks scattered around the house as if conducting important business. One of them swatted a chicken with his stick and laughed as the bird flew up to the roof in a cloud of feathers and angry squawking.

Big Choi faced Yoona in the courtyard of the house.

"As you may know, things have changed in the valley. Yoona, you either resist the change or you can be a part of it," said Big Choi.

Big Choi held Yoona's hands with a strong grip. He made a motion as if to kiss Yoona.

"I cannot, I will not," cried out Yoona as she resisted.

Big Choi's face grew dark. He pushed away Yoona and smashed a jar that was sitting nearby with his sword. One of the boys looked into the courtyard from a doorway.

"Chanho, bring the others back in," said Big Choi.

Soon the boys with bamboo sticks were back in the courtyard.

Big Choi marched into the study room and came back out with a pile of papers. He dumped the papers on the dirt floor of the courtyard. Big Choi went back inside and came out with more papers. Yoona's father was right behind him this time.

"Son, what are you doing?" Yoona's father asked in a calm but firm voice.

"Teacher, this is for your own good," said Big Choi.

Yoona's father looked around the courtyard. The boys held their bamboo sticks before them, the sharp ends pointed at Yoona's father.

"What is the meaning of this?" said Yoona's father.

Big Choi whispered something to the nearest boy, who ran off into the kitchen. Soon the boy came back holding a small pot full of burning embers.

"The northerners have respect for the farmers and workers because they grow food and make useful things. However, they are suspicious of men who do not work with their hands," said Big Choi.

Big Choi took the pot of embers and dumped it on the papers. The papers caught fire and started burning.

"Big Choi, please," cried out Yoona. She rushed to save the papers. One of the boys grabbed Yoona's arms and held her back. The flames burned bright for awhile and then died down.

Without a word, Big Choi and his group of boys gathered up their weapons and left Yoona's house. Yoona's father kneeled on the ground and stared blankly at the ashes and charred scraps of paper that blew about the courtyard like dead leaves.

Chapter 22

For the past couple days Yoona had been worried about her father. Ever since the incident with the burned papers, he seemed changed. Big Choi had destroyed writings Yoona's father had been working on for years. Histories, poems, scholarly commentary. All gone in an instant.

Yoona's father barely touched the food she brought him. Instead, he would nibble a bit of rice and mumble a line from an obscure Chinese poem.

Yoona's father often sat in front of a blank piece of paper with a brush in hand. After a couple brush strokes, he would stop and not write for the rest of the day.

One day Yoona sat quietly in a corner of the study observing her father. She had just brought him some food.

"Appa, do you remember when you told me I should get married soon?"

"Yes, my love."

"And you thought that Big Choi was a good match. He comes from a good family after all."

Yoona's father nodded.

"And these times are so uncertain and dangerous, a girl and her family needs to be protected by a more powerful family," said Yoona.

Yoona's father nodded again.

Yoona paused. She took a deep breath. "So perhaps it would be a good idea for me to marry Big Choi?"

Yoona's father looked at her with his sad and gentle eyes. "Well Yoona, if that makes you happy and Big Choi is the one in your heart."

Yoona winced. She felt a little disappointed. Yoona had hoped that her father would show a stronger response to her proposal, whether he was opposed to it or found it agreeable.

"But you do think it is the best decision, appa?"

"Whatever you wish, Yoona."

"Oh appa," said Yoona. She poured her father a cup of tea. Yoona wondered what to do about her father's sagging spirits.

The next day Yoona was fetching some water from the well when she saw an unfamiliar man walking down the road. He had a shaved head and wore the robes of a monk.

"My child, could you spare a thirsty man some water?" asked the man.

Yoona ladled out the water and the man received it in his hands.

"It is a strange state of affairs these days. I could not enter this valley until I showed a group of young boys I carried no weapons," said the man.

"Do you travel from afar?" asked Yoona.

"I have travelled so much I am both far from and near everywhere."

"Where are you headed?"

"A place that many have searched for but few have reached," said the man.

Yoona frowned. The man seemed to speak in riddles.

"What do you suggest to help a person who has lost everything?" Yoona asked.

"Hope, that is all that's left."

The man looked at the distant mountains, deep in thought. "But these days even hope seems to be in short supply. A dark cloud has descended on our land," continued the man.

"Is it true the northerners have defeated the Korean king and his army?" asked Yoona. She had overheard farmers at the well talking about how Kaesong was overrun by a barbarian army.

"The king managed to escape to Hanyang. The blessings of heaven still shine on the hills to the south of here."

Yoona thought about Mina and her mother in Hanyang.

"Thank you, sir. That sounds like a bit of good news," said Yoona to the man.

The man put the palms of his hands together and bowed to Yoona. He was soon on his way to whatever destination he was seeking.

Yoona drew some more water from the well and made her way home. As she crossed a pasture, Yoona saw the mule that Mina's father had left behind. One of the farmers used it for farm work but otherwise the animal spent his days sleeping and grazing.

An idea started to hatch in Yoona's head.

Chapter 23

The next day Yoona was with her father in his study room.

She had barely slept the night before. Yoona had tossed and turned in bed as she thought over the dangers and difficulties of what she would suggest to her father. Yet if she did not act, Yoona felt her father would fall into an irreversible decline. It was as though Yoona's father was becoming a ghost.

"Appa, I was wondering . . ." said Yoona.

Yoona's father nodded in response as he thumbed through the few papers that did not get burned.

"Appa, I heard Hanyang remains safe from the northerners," said Yoona. She wondered what to say next.

"Appa, remember you told us of when you visited

Hanyang for the summer as a boy?"

Yoona looked intently at her father's face. She was searching and hoping for a spark of light in her father's eyes.

"You told us you had never seen so many temples and schools in your life. One could spend a lifetime reading all the books in the temples. Once your father got angry with you because he couldn't find you. It turned out you were hiding in a temple all day, lost in a world of ancient books."

The faintest smile appeared on Yoona's father's face. "Yes, I remember. That was so long ago."

"And Mina is already there with her mother."

Yoona's father had a faraway look in his eyes. "I remember that summer. My father had official business to attend to, so he brought all of us. We lived in a villa for the summer and met so many noble families from all over Korea."

"Appa, let's go to Hanyang."

"Yes, let's go to Hanyang," said Yoona's father. A little bit of the spark had returned to his eyes.

Yoona spent the next several days thinking about the escape out of the valley. The main roads were guarded at all times by the barbarian warriors. Roadblocks of fallen timbers blocked access at strategic locations.

The boys that followed Big Choi patrolled the hills during the daytime. Although the boys went back to their homes after sunset, the steep and narrow trails in the hills were almost impossible to navigate in the darkness of the night.

Yoona wondered what lay beyond the familiar hills of the valley. She had never travelled that far from her home.

Yoona heard that even in times of peace bandits ambushed travelers on the roads. And the forest was filled with wild animals. Perhaps even tigers. Yoona shuddered at that last thought.

Yoona gathered up enough supplies for the journey. She tied together cloth bundles of food and clothing. Yoona asked the farmer how to handle and take care of the mule.

Yoona felt everything was ready. She just had to wait a couple days for one final and important detail.

Chapter 24

Today was the day. The mule was fully loaded and grazing in the back of the house.

Yoona cooked a final pot of rice in the hearth before the fire died and turned to ashes. She bundled up her sister for the trip and made sure her father was dressed properly too. The days were getting warmer but sometimes a cold rain would fall from the skies.

It was a clear day with no clouds and it seemed the sun would never set. The plan was to leave under the cover of darkness through the hills. Yoona had spent so much time gathering plants in the hills she was familiar with every nook and cranny, at least during the daytime.

The sun finally started to sink in the west behind the hills. It seemed as though the hills were glowing like the dying embers of a hearth. Farmers cast long shadows across the fields as they walked back home.

A group of barbarians on horseback dashed through the fields and village streets, using sticks to pass back and forth among themselves the carcass of a small animal.

Yoona heard the laughter of little children as they played on a mound of grass and dirt. It could have been a scene from when the valley had known peace, except the pile of dirt was where a farmhouse had stood recently.

The gray evening faded into night but the twilight lingered. A full moon was shining brightly. Yoona had waited for this night.

All was quiet. The world had finally settled in for the night. The only sound was that of crickets chirping beneath the house.

Yoona closed all the chests and shuttered all the doors in the house. The chickens that used to peck and scratch the dirt inside the courtyard were either seized by the barbarians or sold off.

"Okay, let's go," Yoona told her father and Yuni in a soft voice. Yuni whimpered quietly in response. The three of them walked behind the house. The mule was resting on the ground.

Yoona grabbed the rope holding the mule and gave it a

tug. The animal reluctantly got up. The entire group entered the woods behind the house.

Yoona gave one final look over her shoulder. She was leaving the house she had grow up in. The place was now empty of all the life, laughter and conversation that used to fill the dwelling.

The path that led away from the house grew steeper. Yoona was familiar with the way but in the darkness of night rocks and exposed tree roots seemed to be everywhere. Yoona's father carried Yuni on his back while Yoona pulled the mule behind her.

After a long climb Yoona found herself on a hilltop.

Down below in the valley numerous camp fires burned where Mina's family estate was located. The northern barbarians preferred sleeping in the open under their rough shelters of animal skin instead of the Korean houses. They had a bad habit though of pulling the paper and wood doors from the buildings for firewood.

Yoona wished she was back home, settled comfortably in her futon with Yuni by her side. By this time she would be shutting her eyes and her father would already be asleep in the next room.

But Yoona knew they had to get away as far as possible from the valley. Perhaps in the coming days Yoona and her family could travel in the daytime but tonight they had to travel under cover of darkness.

Yoona looked into the distance. The full moon illuminated the dark outlines of the hills and mountains that seemed to stretch forever.

Yoona began to realize how long and difficult the journey was going to be and she began to tremble. Yoona wondered if it was possible to turn back. What if she collapsed into her father's arms, crying?

Yoona reminded herself why they were setting out on this journey in the first place. Hanyang. They had to reach Hanyang. That was the goal, to cling to the hope of a brighter tomorrow.

Yoona breathed in deeply and continued ahead with her father and Yuni. The woods were often quite thick and almost pitch dark. Other times the light of the full moon filtered through the trees and illuminated the path before them.

Soon the group was going up and down a series of hills. Going down a hill was more difficult than going up. It was easy to trip on a tree root and go tumbling down.

At one point the path hugged a steep hillside with a sharp drop into rocks on one side and a wall of rock on the other. The mule refused to go any further. Yoona slowly coaxed the animal and gently pulled on its rope.

Yuni got off her father's back. The two linked hands and inched down the path.

❧

Yoona's family and the mule travelled through the rugged landscape for what seemed like a long time. The valley and the home they had left behind was far away now. Yuni was already closing her eyes and nodding off.

"Yoona, let's rest here for now," said Yoona's father. A clearing of trees was before them. A wall of rocks provided shelter.

Yoona agreed to the proposal.

Yoona found a spot near the rocks covered with soft pine needles. She untied the blankets and straw mats the mule was carrying. Soon the three were settled under the blankets. There was a slight chill in the night air but the skies were clear. The stars twinkled overhead.

It was quiet in the woods. The only sounds were that of Yoona's father and Yuni breathing deeply in their sleep. Yoona wondered what lay ahead. Hope was all that was left, thought Yoona as she remembered what the wandering man had told her.

Chapter 25

The next morning Yoona woke up with a start. The sun was in her eyes. For a moment Yoona forgot where she was, as though everything had been a dream. Then it came back to her: the barbarians on horses, the burning houses, the crying of children.

Yoona's father and Yuni were still sleeping. Yoona gathered stones and firewood. She had never cooked outdoors but she imagined it was like building a fire in the hearth.

Yoona had packed for the journey a sack of rice, a cooking pot and a jar for water, among other things. She arranged the wood in a pile and managed to get a smoky fire burning. Soon the pot of rice was steaming and bubbling on the fire.

We are like the northerners with the heavens our roof and the earth our bed, thought Yoona.

Yoona wondered what it would be like to live a nomadic life on horseback. She thought about the prince and wondered where he was now. What was it like to sail across the seas and find a new home in a foreign land?

We are like the prince who lost everything and wandered far from his home, thought Yoona.

Just as the rice was done, Yoona's father and Yuni woke up with a yawning and stretching of limbs. After finishing their morning business the two joined Yoona.

Yoona noticed her father was eating the rice with gusto and she felt happy. She hoped Yuni wouldn't notice that all they had to eat was rice. Yoona had convinced her sister the trip was an adventure to go see their cousin Mina.

Yoona left her sister and father alone to survey the land. She knew they were supposed to travel in a southerly direction to reach Hanyang. But the exact route was unclear.

Yoona climbed atop a rock. Mountains and steep hills stretched as far as she could see. It was rugged terrain but safer than the lowlands.

Yoona made her way back to the campsite. Her father was telling Yuni a story from the heroic age of Korean history. Yoona smiled. She was happy her father was in good spirits.

Yoona packed the bedding and food back on the mule. A long day of traveling lay ahead.

The group had hiked the entire morning. Yoona noticed the path was gently sloping down as she and her family made their way south. The hilly ridges were merging into the lowlands. A great plain with a river running through it lay ahead.

Clusters of farmhouses dotted the plain. From a distance everything looked serene. Beyond the plain in the distance was the beginning of another small mountain range.

Yoona had never seen such a vast expanse of flatland before. The valley Yoona called home could fit many times inside the land that lay ahead.

Yoona looked at the hills and mountains that lay on the other side and guessed it would take the rest of the day to reach it. It was like crossing a big lake to reach the other shore.

The group was soon exiting the hills and traveling on flat ground. The first cluster of farmhouses came into view. A quiet stillness hung in the air.

"Hello?" Yoona called out and was greeted by silence. A

couple of chickens scratched the dirt of a vegetable garden.

The three travelled further.

The rice fields were flooded and planted with rows of transplanted seedlings. Raised dirt paths separated the numerous fields. Walls of stone and earth surrounded farmhouses with thatched roofs. The entire valley was a prosperous farming area except for the strange absence of any people.

Yoona then saw something that was horrifying.

"Yuni, don't look!" Yoona cried out as she clamped her hands over her sister's eyes.

An immense plain of grass was ahead of them. It appeared to be swarmed by crows and vultures that cawed and flapped their wings as they fought for scraps. The birds were so numerous they appeared to be one living, seething mass that covered the land.

Yoona led the mule down the path, followed by her father who held Yuni's hand.

Yuni wore a blindfold Yoona had managed to quickly put over her eyes. The thing Yoona was trying to prevent her sister from seeing was the sight of skulls and rib cages getting furiously torn apart by the birds.

A great battle had been fought here recently. Helmets and

suits of armor were scattered about like the empty shells of insects. Sometimes the path was blocked and the scavenging birds would retreat at the last minute with a flapping of wings as Yoona and her family approached them.

The plain seemed to go on forever.

Yoona felt she was going to collapse and cry uncontrollably but she held on. She gave her father another piece of cloth to put over Yuni's nose and mouth. Fortunately the recent spring plantings meant the rice fields were heavily fertilized by the farmers and the smell of the fertilized rice fields overwhelmed everything.

Finally the three reached the river. Yoona took off her sandals and dipped her toes in the water. The river was wide but shallow and its waters clean and refreshing.

Yoona's father took off the blinds covering Yuni's face and soon the group made its way across the river.

A small village lay on the other side. The streets were empty and devoid of life. Some of the houses were piles of rubble and charred wood.

Yoona and her family traveled through the village and scavenged among the standing houses for food. By the time they were done the mule was loaded with a couple chickens, vegetables and extra clothing. Yoona felt bad about taking everything but the long-gone villagers did not need their possessions anymore.

More rice fields stretched beyond the village walls. Numerous green seedlings stood in ankle-deep water that was the color of mud.

An overturned ox cart lying in middle of the road hinted at the swift and violent nature of the battle. Valuable farming tools lay scattered about. Dark-feathered birds circled overhead occasionally. The rest of the valley looked quite peaceful, with cherry blossoms in full bloom lining the side of the road.

Empty farmhouses dotted the landscape. Sparrows were already making homes underneath the thatch roofs. Yoona wondered if her house back in the valley was falling into such a state of natural decay. She imagined grass growing in the courtyard and a tree sapling peeking out of a crack in the walls.

Yoona had a mental image of Big Choi tearing and raging through the house when he discovered that Yoona and her family had fled. She shuddered a little and walked faster. The hills in the distance were getting closer.

The bright sun of high noon was waning when Yoona and her family finally made their way to the foothills. Yoona had never before felt so relieved to see the land rise up into rugged hills and mountains before her.

The group hiked deep into the hills and did not stop until the sun started to set.

Finally Yoona stood on a lookout point and gazed back at the valley she had left. From a distance it looked so peaceful, a lush and fertile place bordered by mountains and watered by a wide and lazy river. Yoona wondered if she would ever forget the sights she had seen there.

Yoona's father suggested a protected rocky alcove as a good resting spot for the night and here the three concluded their day's journey.

Chapter 26

Yoona and her family spent the next couple days journeying through the mountains. The terrain was rugged and progress was often slow. At times the lowlands came into view on either side of the mountain range but Yoona knew it was risky to venture there.

Yoona was glad the group had not encountered dangerous animals such as wolves or bears. She remembered the birds scavenging on the plain. Perhaps the wolves were in the lowlands, thought Yoona.

As for bears, Yoona's father often sang loudly or banged a small gong he had found in the empty village to warn them. Her father explained to Yoona that bears were quite shy and did not wish to encounter humans.

Yoona's father told her and Yuni how the Korean

people were descended from a bear who wished to assume human form and was granted this wish by the heavens. Yoona thought it would be good to be a bear and live in the woods, living off roots and berries.

The weather had been balmy and warm until today.

As the day progressed the temperature dropped steadily. The clouds darkened and a chilly rain started to fall, a trickle that became a deluge. The group tried to find shelter under the trees but the wind blew sheets of rain directly at them.

By nightfall the rain had become a light drizzle but everything was soaked, including the clothes, food and bedding.

Yoona and her father tried to build a fire but all they could manage was a smoky and smoldering mess that barely warmed them.

Yoona hung the clothes and bedding on tree branches to dry. Yoona huddled with her father and sister under the driest straw matting and bedding they had and slept in fits and starts until the next morning.

The next morning Yoona woke up shivering. The clothes on the trees were covered with a fine dusting of frost. The fire was a cold pile of ashes and unburnt logs.

Yoona gathered all the dry wood she could find and

managed to build a campfire.

"Everyone, wake up. It's time to eat," said Yoona after the rice was finished.

A weak moan came from Yuni. "Unni, it hurts," she said.

"Yuni, what's the matter?" asked Yoona. She rushed over to her sister. Yuni's lips were blue and her face was as white as a cotton sheet.

"Yuni, oh Yuni, please get better," cried Yoona as she rubbed her sister's limbs.

Yoona rushed back to the pot of boiling rice and tossed in some herbal roots she had found in the deserted village. After it was done, Yoona fed the food to her sister. Yuni could barely eat the food before vomiting.

Yoona's father sat helpless. Yoona felt helpless too. She felt her little sister was slipping away from her. But Yoona realized she couldn't just sit there and cry about it.

Yoona walked over to the supplies and tossed out extra bedding and even a heavy sack of potatoes. She loaded up the remaining effects back on the mule. Yoona had her father hoist Yuni on top of the mule.

"Let's go, appa," said Yoona. Yoona wasn't sure of the day's destination exactly but she felt they had to move fast and with purpose.

After eating breakfast the group was back on the

mountain trail. Yuni was lying stomach down on the mule's back, her eyes shut and limbs hanging downward.

Yoona and her family had been traveling through the mountains for most of the day.

Yuni remained on the mule in the same position as in the morning. She could barely eat the food given her. The weather remained chilly and the skies were the color of slate. Hope is all that's left, thought Yoona as the group travelled through a thickly-wooded area.

The forest opened up into a clearing. Down below was a narrow valley. The valley was inhabited. Farmhouses hugged the sides of the mountain and rice fields were terraced into ledges.

The path into the valley was steep and rocky. Yoona's father carried Yuni on his back while Yoona guided the mule down. Yoona was wary of venturing into populated areas but she had to, for her sister's sake.

Chapter 27

Yoona and her family passed the first farmhouse. The place was tidy in appearance with a freshly-thatched roof. Firewood was neatly stacked against the walls. A modest flowerbed provided a splash of color.

Further down the hill, other farmhouses came into view.

Yoona was thinking what an odd sight they probably made, a girl leading a mule followed by her father.

A child appeared. The little boy saw Yoona, laughed and ran away. Soon a crowd of children descended on the group. Yoona was struck by how full of joy they all seemed. The children laughed and peppered Yoona with questions. Soon their mothers appeared.

"Aigoo, where did such pretty girls come from?" asked

one of the mothers.

"Oh, but what's the matter with the younger one?"

Yoona's father explained Yuni's situation.

"The poor girl," all the women exclaimed. One of them, an old grandmother, invited Yoona's family into her house. A futon was prepared in a small room and soon Yuni was resting comfortably.

The old woman who had invited Yoona and her father fussed over Yoona as if she was her own child. She set a table with a generous amount of food and drinks and insisted the two eat as much as possible.

As Yoona and her father ate, the other mothers and village children looked at them from outside the open screen doors of the dining room.

Soon the men came in from the fields and stared at the visitors and talked amongst themselves.

Suddenly the chatter stopped and the crowd made way for an old man. He was dressed in robes and had a flowing white beard. Everyone bowed their heads. Yoona and her father got up from their eating, kneeled and bowed to the old man.

"I hear there is a sick child here," said the old man.

Yoona's father led the old man to Yuni's room. The old man kneeled beside Yuni. He held her hand and touched her forehead. The old man opened a pouch by his side and pulled out some herbal medicine.

"A slight fever and chilling of the body," said the old man. "She should recover in a couple days."

Yoona's father bowed deeply in gratitude. The old man went back to the dining room and sat down.

"Let us continue this meal my wife has prepared for us. Please tell me from where you come and where you are headed," said the old man.

Yoona realized the old man was the village elder. The other villagers continued to gawk from outside at the scene inside the house.

Yoona's father told the old man how the northern barbarians were waging war against the Koreans.

"War? This valley has not known war since I was a little boy and that was a long time ago," said the old man.

Yoona's father asked whether the villagers were aware the Korean king had fled Kaesong in the face of the enemy invasion.

"News from the outside world reaches us like a seed dropped by a sparrow as it flies over a field. That is, once in a while," said the old man.

Yoona's father noted the isolated location of the valley.

"Yes, we are far from many things. But we have everything we need here. Water and sunshine to grow our crops and just enough land to live on. The younger sons sometimes venture out in search of new land to farm but otherwise we've been happy here for many generations," said the old man.

Yoona's father nodded. Yoona ate her food silently and listened in on the conversation.

"The oldest one, she is of an age to be married?" asked the old man in the blunt manner typical of many Koreans.

"Yes. If you know of any eldest sons with a good plot of land, she is available," said Yoona's father.

Yoona felt her face flush.

"Excellent! Make yourselves at home in my house. The youngest one needs plenty of rest and good medicine," said the old man.

By the time Yoona and her father finished their meal the sun had set. The villagers had long dispersed, their curiosity satisfied. Yoona and her father settled into a room next to Yuni's. As she settled into the futon, Yoona realized it was the first time in many nights she was sleeping under a roof.

The next morning Yoona woke up. She started to run through her head the things she needed to do such as lighting a cooking fire.

Yoona paused. The smell of a wood fire wafted through

the house. The sound of an old woman humming to herself carried from the kitchen. Yoona put on her slippers and made her way to the kitchen.

"Good morning, I hope you slept well. Can I help you?" asked Yoona when she saw the old woman in the kitchen stirring a pot.

"Oh no, my child. Stay in bed a little longer. You are a guest in the house," said the old woman as she gently shooed Yoona out of the kitchen.

Yoona checked on her sister Yuni. She was sleeping soundly.

A little later the old woman called for everyone to eat. The knee-high table in the dining room was spread out with a variety of foods including eggs, soup and various fruits.

Yoona felt lighthearted because she was so used to waking up early in the morning to make sure the food was prepared.

After breakfast Yoona decided to venture out into the valley. The food she ate had been plentiful and delicious. Everything was grown or raised on the nearby farms.

The total acreage of fertile land in the small valley was sparse but every piece of ground was meticulously cultivated. Fruit trees grew on the slopes of the mountains in perfect rows. The spring rice seedlings grew in carefully constructed terraces that were flooded with water. Every farmhouse had a well-tended vegetable garden.

Yoona walked down a narrow dirt path that led to a pasture. Sheep grazed there.

"Hello," said a young boy.

"Oh hello," said Yoona. She felt her pulse quicken. The boy looked to be about Yoona's age. He was holding a stick used to herd the sheep. He was dressed simply in white cotton trousers and shirt and was barefoot.

"My name is Youngmin. I saw you arrive yesterday with your family."

"My name is Yoona. Pleased to meet you."

Yoona smiled at the boy, turned around and ran back to the house. She spent the rest of the day inside helping to mend wicker baskets and straw sandals.

Chapter 28

Yuni's recovery was slow but steady. Every day the old man prepared a medicinal broth that he gave to Yoona to serve to Yuni. Yuni would grimace and twist her face and finally swallow the bitter medicine.

Yoona spent her days helping with the chores around the farmhouse. Her father spent his time discussing Korean history and Chinese poetry with the old man.

Every day after Yoona finished her chores she would go walking in the hills and meet the shepherd boy Youngmin. Since their initial meeting Yoona had gotten closer to him.

Youngmin was the grandson, or rather one of the many grandsons, of the old man. He knew all the hidden corners and paths in the valley. Yoona and Youngmin would spend entire afternoons exploring the place.

Youngmin had never left the valley and Yoona would tell him about the things she had seen before meeting him. Yoona felt as though she was a foreigner landing on a distant shore after a great journey.

Yoona remembered a certain prince who had come from a distant shore. She felt a dull aching in her chest when she thought of the prince. Where was he now? Yoona wondered if what Big Choi said about foolish hopes for an unknown future was true.

One day Yoona was outside with her father. The rice fields in the valley grew like a lush green carpet. When Yoona and her family had arrived in the valley, the fields had been muddy pools with seedlings poking their scrawny shoots out of the water.

The day was sunny and Yoona's sister was playing with a group of children her age that had befriended her. It seemed the war and destruction Yoona had witnessed was a faint memory.

"Yoona, this place is a valley of happiness, is it not?" said Yoona's father.

"Yes, appa."

"It seems so far from the cares of the outside world. And Yuni is happy and healthy again."

Yoona nodded.

"The Honorable Elder said it would be good to have a teacher educate the young boys of the valley," continued Yoona's father. "Did you know that boy Youngmin is his favorite grandson, Yoona?"

"I didn't know that," said Yoona.

"Yes, he's a nice young man," said Yoona's father. He seemed to be deep in thought.

Yoona's father continued, "Yoona, my pretty one, our lives are short. Yet we are always dreaming of a happier future. But sometimes the present is where that happiness lies."

Yoona was walking with her father past an orchard of apple trees. One of the younger saplings was tied to a wooden stake. Yoona imagined that she was like a sapling, taking root in the soil of the valley.

Yoona saw another tree in the orchard, an ancient tree with gnarled branches that were twisted. She wondered what it would be like to take root in the valley, flourish and grow old, surrounded by children and grandchildren, with her former life in the valley of her childhood a distant memory.

It should have been a happy thing to contemplate but Yoona felt there was something missing. But she couldn't put a finger on it.

Chapter 29

The next day Yoona and Youngmin walked together in the rugged hills surrounding the valley. The valley was sweet in its isolation and blessed with fertile soil. A stream gurgled down from the mountains and watered the place.

Yoona greatly enjoyed Youngmin's company. He was knowledgeable about the rare plants of the valley that grew in hidden spots.

Youngmin told Yoona about the local spirits that lived in the mountains and brought good fortune to the place. Yoona felt as though she was one with the spirits of the valley. The past and future of the place was her past and future. The two rested on a rocky ledge that overlooked the valley.

"See that grove of trees over there near my father's

house?" said Youngmin as he pointed into the distance.

Yoona nodded.

"We're planning on clearing that land to grow more rice and add another room to the house," said Youngmin. "A room for me and eventually . . . a family."

Youngmin took Yoona's hand in his own. The two sat on the rock in silence.

Fog shrouded the mountains in the distance. It was as though the world outside the valley was a mirage. What was real was the rock Yoona was sitting on and the warmth of Youngmin's hand in her hand.

"Youngmin, do you believe in hope for the future?"

"What do you mean?"

"You believe that something will happen in the future. Or somebody promises you something, so you hope. But then the future is here and you wonder if your hope was an illusion," said Yoona.

"I don't know. I guess I just live in the present. I'm happy when the rain is plentiful and the grass is growing green for my sheep."

Yoona thought that would be good. Just live in the present, she thought.

Yoona eventually made her way down back to the village with Youngmin. The two reached a fork in the road.

"I guess it's time for goodbye," said Yoona.

"Until tomorrow," answered Youngmin with a smile.

"Yes, yes, until tomorrow!" said Yoona as the two embraced. Tomorrow was the next day and tomorrow Yoona was going to see Youngmin, as sure as the rising of the sun.

Yoona walked back to the old man's house where she was staying with a lightness in her step.

Yoona saw her father and the old man in the courtyard. Yoona's father was drawing Chinese characters in the loose sand with a stick and explaining them to the old man.

Yoona then realized it. No one in the valley could read or write.

Yoona went inside the house after greeting her elders. She mulled over her new discovery.

The people in the valley didn't really need to read or write. Their lives were one of farming and raising sheep. Life had gone on for generations without any need to write or read complex hanja characters. The farmers in Yoona's home valley had no use for writing, too.

Yoona thought about the old man's wooden medicine cabinet with its many tiny drawers. Every one of them held a healing root or herb. The villagers would show up at the old man's house whenever someone had a fever or ache. Yoona thought the old man was very wise as he opened up the various drawers and mixed up a healing potion.

The old man *was* infinitely wise in his own way, thought Yoona.

Though he could not read or write, the old man had lived long and knew what was in the hearts of men and women. He was a storehouse of the valley's history, passed from one generation to another. The farmers came to him for advice on many matters, from the best location for a drainage ditch to the season's prospects for a good rain.

Yoona remembered her father's greatest joy back home was spending the afternoon drinking rice wine with the other noblemen and writing calligraphy.

"Yoona, a wise man's mind is like the heavens and its countless stars. To read his writings is like touching those stars," Yoona's father once told her.

Yoona's father finally came into the bedroom.

"Appa, I was wondering about something."

"Yes, my love?"

"Appa, you asked me a couple days ago whether I was happy here."

"I think I did."

"Are you happy here, appa?"

Yoona's father winced, so slightly it was like a flicker of shadow and light on his face. "I am as happy as I can ever be," he answered.

"But appa, what if you have to forget all you had hoped for?"

"Life can take strange turns, Yoona. The path of life may lead us in a direction we hadn't anticipated. And besides, I am old. What is best for you and your sister is what is best for me."

"We were on the way to Hanyang before we came here. Remember you told us how as a boy you spent days lost in the temples of Hanyang, reading ancient books?"

Yoona's father had a distant look in his eyes, as if he was looking back to that long-gone happy summer.

"Gomo and Mina are there," said Yoona.

Yoona's father looked into the distance again. "Hanyang, Hanyang . . ." he repeated softly to himself, as if the word was a mantra.

Chapter 30

The mule was loaded with fresh bedding, clothes and food. Yoona, her father and Yuni were on the path leading out of the valley. The entire village was gathered around them, young and old. Everyone was there except for one person.

Old grandmothers pushed fruit and other pieces of food into Yoona's hands but her attention was somewhere else. Yoona looked frantically over the heads of the villagers gathered around her and her family.

Youngmin, where are you, thought Yoona.

The past few days had been a frantic blur. Yoona's father finally came around to the idea of resuming the journey to Hanyang.

Yoona broke the news to Youngmin of her family

leaving the valley. Youngmin had pleaded with Yoona to stay.

Yoona cried. Youngmin stormed and brooded. Yoona asked him to leave the valley with her. Youngmin could not imagine such a thing. Yoona cried again.

Yoona's father was talking to the old man. Yuni was exchanging little flowers and colorful pebbles with the village children. The mule was slowly chewing a piece of fruit that had fallen on the ground.

Meanwhile Yoona's eyes darted over the hills and rooftops and fields. Youngmin was nowhere to be found.

"So we shall now make our way to Hanyang," said Yoona's father to the old man as they exchanged farewells with each other. The children in the village bowed in unison to Yoona's father and shouted out their farewells.

Manseh! Manseh! Ten thousand years!

Yoona and her family made their way up the path with the mule. The path grew steeper and rockier. The valley behind them receded into the distance and the farmhouses became smaller and smaller.

The crowd of villagers was still gathered and watching the departure of Yoona's family. The individuals became blurred, like tiny figures in a painting.

Yoona tried to hold back but soon tears streamed down

her cheeks.

Chapter 31

Yoona and her family had been traveling in the mountains for about four days and making good progress. The villagers of the valley had provided them with plenty of food and the weather was mild.

Yoona noticed large and well-populated settlements were becoming more frequent in sight. Sometimes the party encountered farmers gathering firewood or medicinal herbs in the mountains. The locals were helpful in pointing the way to Hanyang.

Ever since leaving the place her father called a valley of happiness, Yoona often thought of the time she had spent there. She wondered in her heart if she and her family lost a sort of simple and lasting happiness that comes rarely in life.

Yoona wondered if she could ever find the valley again. After leaving the place Yoona and her family had taken many a twisting and forked path through the mountains. It was as though the valley was swallowed up by the countless hills and mountains that seemed to blur into one.

Yoona was deep in thought when Yuni cried out.

"Look! Down below!"

The group had just crested a small mountain. Before them was a large plain crowded with enough houses to fill a thousand villages. Slender pagodas rose up among the sea of roofs.

A walled compound of tiled-roof buildings dominated the heart of the valley. A magnificent river ran east and west across the place. On the opposite bank of the river grew rice fields that shimmered like an emerald sea.

Yoona had just laid her eyes on Hanyang.

Yoona and her family made their way down the mountain. Soon they were on a main road that led up to a city gate. The gatehouse was constructed of heavy timbers with a stone base and a tiled roof.

A sloping wall of packed earth rose up on both sides of the gatehouse. The massive wall was wide enough for a man with a horse to walk on top of it. Soldiers wearing colorful uniforms and armed with pikes guarded the gate.

The gate doors were wide open and a steady stream of people passed through it, mostly farmers carrying loads of vegetables and firewood.

Yoona felt the excitement rising in her as she and her family approached the gate. The opening of the gate appeared very tall and wide close-up, as if it was made for a giant man.

Soon Yoona was passing through the dark tunnel-like interior of the gatehouse. The doors were made of thick wood and reinforced with cast iron bits.

A flood of smells and sounds hit Yoona as she and her family emerged into the settlement behind the walls.

Crowds of people and animals jostled past Yoona. The streets seemed to go in every direction and were filled with storefronts selling everything from cloth to a scholar's brushes. The wooden buildings lining the streets were tightly packed together and some of them even rose up to three floors.

A man in a doorway shouted "Fresh roasted chestnuts!" to anyone that passed by. A mouth-watering smell of roasted chestnuts mingled with burning coals wafted out from his store.

Yoona's father appeared to be as bewildered as Yoona by the assault on the senses. After a while he recovered himself. "Bukchon, I believe that's where we stayed," said Yoona's father.

Yoona's father stopped a passerby and asked for directions. The passerby waved his hands excitedly and talked fast as he explained the way to Yoona's father. The people of this place even talked in a different manner, thought Yoona.

Yoona and her family made their way through the crowded streets with the mule. Yoona's father bought her and Yuni red bean cakes from a street vendor.

Yoona took in the street scene unfolding before her eyes as she walked and nibbled the red bean cake.

Little children dashed through the dirt of the streets. Fish vendors dumped their trash into roadside ditches for stray cats to pounce on. A nobleman dressed in fine clothes passed by with a haughty air, as if the people surrounding him were little children bothering him.

After some walking, the Yoona and her family found themselves in a quiet neighborhood. Walled villas were crowded together on a steep hill. Most of the villas were almost twice as large as Yoona's house back home but occupied smaller plots of land.

"Yoona and Yuni, we are now in Bukchon. This neighborhood is where my family stayed one summer when I was a little boy," said Yoona's father. "Mina's father has a place here."

Yoona's father stopped an elderly gentleman for directions. The man had a flowing white beard, wore a scholar's hat and was dressed simply but elegantly. Yoona's father asked him if he knew where the distinguished governor's house was and the gentleman pointed up the hill.

Yoona and Yuni followed their father past several more villas. High stone walls concealed the houses. Only tiled rooftops and an occasional tall tree were visible from the street. Yoona's father walked up to a gate and knocked on the solid wood doors.

"Who is it?" asked a female voice.

"My dear sister, it is me," said Yoona's father.

The door opened.

"Gomo!" cried the two girls as they hugged their aunt.

"Aigoo, such a long time. Yuni has grown so much since the last time I saw her and Yoona is prettier than ever. Everyone come in please," said Gomo.

Leaving the dusty streets and stepping inside the walls of the villa was like entering a different world.

Most of the space inside the walls was taken up by the main house. A garden filled with tender blooms and neatly-trimmed evergreens took up the remaining open space. Carefully-arranged rocks suggested a mountain range. A small pool of water stocked with fish was the ocean of this miniature world. A veranda wrapped around the main house and faced the garden.

The paper and wood-framed screen doors of the house were left open and revealed elegantly furnished interiors.

A fragrant smell of flowers and polished wood floated in the air. It was a world removed from both the sweaty, noisy streets of the city and the earthy countryside.

"So tell me the latest news from back home," said Gomo. A single female servant was going back and forth to the kitchen and bringing out food and drinks.

Yoona's father told his sister of the invasion of the valley and the long journey to Hanyang.

When his sister asked about her husband the governor, Yoona's father hesitated. He finally broke down and told the story of the governor's house arrest. Gomo started crying. Yoona's father held his sister in a warm embrace.

"All we have is hope," said Yoona's father.

The group resumed the meal. Gomo regained her composure, though she wiped her eyes from time to time.

There was a sound of the front gate opening and closing with a creak followed by a soft thud. Mina appeared in the open doorway of the dining room. She was dressed in modest yet finely-cut clothing.

Yoona had already noticed the local nobles of Hanyang were rather refined in their dress. Yoona felt like a country girl. I *am* a country girl, she thought.

"Good afternoon, uncle," Mina greeted Yoona's father with a bow.

The conversation resumed.

Gomo updated everyone about the war against the northerners.

The Korean army had won some key battles but lost others. The northern defenses had long crumbled. Kaesong was overrun but the king and his ministers were safe in Hanyang. Many ordinary Koreans from all over the land had fled to Hanyang, swelling its population.

After the food was finished and the table cleared, Gomo produced a writing set for Yoona's father. Yoona saw her father's eyes light up at the sight of the paper, brush and ink.

The servant brought out fresh slices of watermelon. Yoona took a slice and retreated to the veranda with Mina and Yuni.

As Yoona bit into the succulent fruit, she heard her father talking to Gomo inside the house. Her father's voice was full of joy and carried into the evening air. He was relating the events of the journey from their home to Hanyang.

Yoona looked at the stones in the garden arranged to look like a mountain. It reminded her of the journey through the endless hills and valleys of the kingdom. She thought of one particular valley, small and yet blessed with fertile land and hidden from the outside world.

Perhaps it is for the best we are here, Yoona thought.

Chapter 32

The next morning Yoona found an empty field near the villa to pasture the mule. It was just a patch of ground but Yoona thought in this place of endless buildings the field may as well have been a vast plain. The mule seemed happy and started eating the grass growing in the field.

Gomo suggested to Mina and Yoona the two girls should go out and explore the city. Yoona couldn't contain her excitement. The neighborhood of villas was on a steep hill and from here Yoona could see the rooftops of the houses before her.

A low-lying mountain sat in the distance. Behind the mountain was the Han River, as the locals called it. Soon Yoona and Mina walked down the hill with small bundles of rice balls and rice cakes to eat during the day.

Mina appeared to be familiar with the streets and

landmarks of Hanyang. She led Yoona down winding alleys. Yoona was so absorbed with all the sights she occasionally stepped into a muddy puddle.

Finally the two girls approached a massive gate that looked similar to the one that had greeted Yoona and her family when they first entered Hanyang. Numerous market stalls surrounded the stone walls of the gate.

"This is the Big Eastern Gate," said Mina. "Many merchants from all over Korea sell their wares here. Some of them are even foreigners from distant lands."

Yoona was struck with wonder by all the goods being sold in the marketplace: cloth, fine furniture, metal tools, shoes.

Yoona heard the jabbering of a foreign language and looked in the direction of the sounds. Two merchants in long flowing robes and beards were arguing. One of them was rapidly moving little beads on an abacus.

A stall in front of the merchants was filled with wooden containers of fragrant spices. Yoona breathed in the sweet and exotic smells as the two girls passed directly by the stall. She could not help but stare at the merchants.

Both of the merchants had pale eyes like those of a fish and their facial features seemed oversize and exaggerated compared to a Korean's. Yoona wondered how far across the ocean the two merchants had travelled.

The two girls walked further.

"Ahead of us, they're Chinese people," said Mina as she gently poked Yoona in the ribs.

An entire alley was lined with stalls overflowing with piles of silk cloth. The merchants looked like Koreans but babbled in a foreign language.

One of the Chinese merchants was showing off a bolt of silk the color of the summer sky to a Korean buyer. The soft material flowed in his hands like water. Yoona thought it would be wonderful to have a dress made from this material.

Yoona and Mina finally left the marketplace. Yoona felt as though she had been transported briefly to a strange land far from Korea. She followed Mina as she made her way down the streets. Soon the two girls encountered an open space with a stream flowing through it.

The water was dirty and fetid.

"Look over there," said Mina as she pointed upstream.

The stream was crowded with families. Naked children splashed in the water while their mothers washed clothes. Flimsy shelters made of wood, paper and fabric clung to both sides of the stream. Smoky cooking fires burned here and there

"Since the war began the population of Hanyang has

doubled in size. Many of the refugees have settled around this stream," said Mina as she wrinkled her nose and quickened her steps.

Yoona remembered not too long ago she and her family were sleeping out in the open and bathing in streams.

The two girls left the stream behind and found themselves walking through a dense maze of narrow alleys. Sometimes the passageways were so narrow Yoona could open her arms and almost touch the walls on either side.

The place was thick with the smells of food and cooking fires. Numerous one-room establishments sold bowls of noodles. Other places were so small there was space only to stand on the street and eat standing up.

A porter carrying a load of firewood on his back went through the alley. Yoona and Mina pressed themselves flat against a wall as the porter walked past them.

The girls walked past a place selling hot bowls of beef broth and noodle soup. The owner was a round-faced woman with red cheeks. She spotted the girls looking at the pot of soup boiling on a fire.

"Did you know that pot has been continuously boiling for almost a week?" said the woman as she skimmed some foam off the top. She added a fresh cup of water.

"Here, try some," said the woman as she gave the girls

two small cups of broth.

Yoona tasted the soup and thought it was good.

Just then a commotion erupted in the alley. A crowd of little children ran past, shouting excitedly. A couple adults followed after them. Soon more children passed by.

Everybody was headed in one direction. Yoona and Mina gulped down their soups, thanked the woman and hurried to see what all the excitement was about.

Yoona found herself rushing down the narrow alleys, turning left and right. Yoona wasn't sure where she and Mina were headed but everyone seemed to be rushing in the same direction. A bright open space was up ahead.

Yoona and Mina burst out of the shadows and into a wide street that was the main east-west boulevard of Hanyang. A large crowd was already gathered. Yoona stood on her toes and jumped up and down to catch a view of the scene unfolding before the crowd.

A small army was making its way down the street. The soldiers wore bloody bandages and had scruffy beards grown long after months in the field. Many of the soldiers carried the marks of recent battle injuries.

A few of the noble officers rode horses but most of the men shuffled their feet and kicked up clouds of fine dust in their wake. The soldiers slung their weapons over their shoulders or dragged them on the ground.

It was an army of broken men passing by.

The crowd lining the street was silent. A temple bell somewhere in the district chimed its somber tones.

Yoona thought back to the time when the noble sons of the valley rode off to war in high spirits. She looked at the tired and gaunt faces of the men passing by and wondered if the prince was in the crowd. Or did the prince meet his end on a desolate and faraway battlefield?

The number of soldiers seemed countless. It seemed quite a while before the flood of men thinned out. A few stragglers in the rear struggled to keep up with their comrades. A couple stray dogs barked and ran after them. The dust clouds kicked up by the soldiers lingered in the air and started to choke Yoona's throat.

Yoona overheard someone in the crowd talking about the most recent defeat of the Korean forces in a large battle. Another person wondered when the northerners would start knocking on the gates of Hanyang. The crowd slowly dispersed and everyone went back to their business.

Yoona and Mina made their way home. Soon the two girls were walking up the hills of Bukchon.

Yoona looked at the mountains in the distance. Stone walls that looked like dragon's teeth ran across some of the mountain ridges. Yoona wondered if even they were enough to keep out the northern barbarians.

Chapter 33

Mina's mother was getting ready to leave the house. She packed a cloth-wrapped bundle of fresh cotton bandages. Gomo had been leaving the house in such a manner for the past couple days and coming back late in the evening, dirtied and exhausted.

Meanwhile Yoona's father spent his days going to one temple or another. The girls stayed alone in the house with the lone servant, who cooked them meals.

"Umma, where are you going?" asked Mina.

"The King of Korea has called on all the mothers to help the nation heal," answered Gomo.

"You mean all those soldiers that arrived in Hanyang a couple days ago?" said Mina.

"Yes. There are so many wounded soldiers they need all

the extra help they can get."

"I want to go help," said Yuni.

"Yuni, you are a little too young, although some of the daughters of the noble families have volunteered their time and efforts," said Gomo.

Yoona and Mina looked at each other.

"I suppose if you girls want to come today, that'll be good. But be forewarned, it's not going to be a pretty sight," said Gomo.

Yoona headed with Mina and her mother to the district of Hanyang where the military camp was located. It was centrally located near a small hill the locals called Yongsan.

After some traveling the three arrived at a large field surrounded by barracks and shelters. The open spaces were filled with countless soldiers resting on the ground. Many of the men were lying motionless as if they were no longer alive.

Gomo handed Yoona and Mina handkerchiefs to put over their mouths.

The summer heat was intense and seemed to intensify all the smells of the place. Moans and cries of pain rose up among the men lying on the ground. Yoona recalled the battlefield she and her family had crossed.

Several wise old men holding bags of healing roots and herbs walked among the soldiers and tended to them. Women followed behind and helped clean up wounds and change bandages.

Another area was devoted to cooking food. Pots big enough to hold a small pig boiled and bubbled with cooking rice. Yoona's mother had Mina and Yoona help distribute the food to the fallen soldiers. The soldiers that could stand were lined up in the cooking area.

Yoona grabbed a sack of rice balls and waded into the sea of men. Some of the men held out their hands while others could barely move their heads. The food went quickly and Yoona had to go back for more rice balls several times.

Yoona walked up to a group of men leaning against a building wall. She was down to her last few rice balls but fortunately there was enough for everyone.

"Yoona," a young man called out to her in a weak voice.

Yoona almost dropped the food. It was the prince.

The prince was sitting on the ground and resting against a building wall. His hair looked like a bird's nest and his face was sunburnt. A few tufts of hair on his chin was all the prince could grow for a beard.

The prince seemed to have no visible injuries. But he

looked exhausted, as though all the life energy was drained out of him.

Yoona held the prince's hands. Her heart was beating wildly.

"Oh Prince Lee!" cried Yoona. The other men nearby looked at Yoona. Yoona felt her face flushing. The prince responded by holding Yoona's hands tighter.

Yoona wanted to collapse into the prince's arms. She felt like an immense cooking pot boiling over, so intense were the feelings inside Yoona at the moment.

"It's been a long time," the prince finally answered.

"Yes, a long time," said Yoona.

The prince appeared to grow weaker. He closed his eyes. An old man walked by and handed Yoona a small cloth bag of roots.

"He has a fever and will get better with time. Give him a pinch of this medicine every couple days," said the old man.

Yoona bowed to the old man. She was now responsible for the prince's care. Yoona put a blanket over the prince and resumed passing out the remaining rice balls.

Chapter 34

Yoona was feeling restless.

She observed Mina's mother playing a game of baduk with her father. Like all proper Korean women, Gomo knew how to play a good game and somehow lose every time she played against a man.

Gomo had not been back to the military camp since the last visit. She explained to the girls that the first hectic days after the soldiers returned to Hanyang was when any available help was needed the most.

Gomo told Yoona she planned on going to the camp soon though. Mina seemed quite content with not having to go back there.

Yoona's father spent most of his days reading books in the numerous temples of Hanyang. He told Gomo how the day before a monk had let him borrow some rare books from China on the Enlightened One's teachings.

Yoona announced to everyone she was going for a walk outside. By now she was familiar with the local streets and general landmarks around Hanyang. Everyone else in the house was busy with their activities and took little notice of Yoona leaving the place.

The world outside the walls of the villa was hot and dusty. The summer sun had baked everything to a dry crisp. Yoona wore a head scarf to protect herself. She walked down the hill with no particular destination in mind.

Yoona looked over the view of Hanyang that stretched before her.

Even after seeing it many times, Yoona felt wonder at the sight of so many countless houses squeezed next to each other. She saw the smoke rising up from the chimneys and wondered what sort of food the busy mothers were cooking in their kitchens.

Temples graced many of the hilltops of Hanyang. When the monks rung the bells a solemn gonging sound carried into the air. Yoona smiled as she thought of her father spending hours inside the dark and cool interior of a temple poring over old books.

Yoona cast her eyes over the general direction of the

military district. The prince was there somewhere, recovering from his fever.

Yoona thought much about the prince lately. It seemed so long ago when they first met. Both Yoona and the prince had taken a long journey and now they were reunited.

Yoona was walking through an unfamiliar district when a smell of animal waste hit her nose. She had been away from the countryside for so long the odor seemed quite overpowering.

A large fenced-in area nearby held a herd of horses. All of the animals appeared to be tired and malnourished. Their rib cages were visible and their hides covered with open sores. Clouds of flies buzzed around. A little boy dressed in rags swatted the horses with a whip-like tree branch as he tried to herd them.

Yoona remembered her fear of horses and hurried past the horse pen. As she walked past the fence, a horse trotted up to her. It was mangy like the others. Yoona instantly recognized the animal.

Toki, thought Yoona. She remembered when the prince's horse ate the vegetables in the garden and she called him Toki, the Korean word for rabbit. Yoona was still afraid of horses but she remembered how Toki and the prince saved her from the tiger.

Yoona reached over and touched Toki.

The horse gently nuzzled Yoona's face. His large brown eyes looked sad.

"Oh Toki, what happened to you?" said Yoona as she hugged the horse's neck.

The little boy came over to Yoona.

"What are you doing? These animals belong to my father."

"Where are they going? What will your father do with them?"

"My father is a butcher. He will kill them for their hides and meat, of course. He bought the whole herd from the Korean army at a good price."

"Oh no!" cried Yoona.

A man walked up to Yoona and the boy. He was dark, lean and muscular and wore a blood-stained apron. He carried two knives, a short curved one and a long one with a big blade.

"What's going on here?" asked the man.

The little boy pointed at Yoona.

"Sir, this horse belonged to a good friend of mine. I was wondering if I can buy it from you," said Yoona.

The man laughed, as if he couldn't believe someone wanted to buy such a tired old animal.

"What do you have in exchange?" asked the man.

Yoona only had a couple copper coins her father had given her. She then remembered the one thing she had that was precious, a jade charm that hung around her neck. It was given to her by her father, who in turn received it from a scholar friend of his who had spent many years in China.

Yoona took off the charm and offered it to the man.

The man laughed again. "What use do I have for such a thing?"

The man then furrowed his brow, as if he was thinking of something. "Come follow me, my highborn young lady," he said to Yoona as he turned around and walked towards a large wooden building.

The interior of the building was dark. Flies buzzed everywhere and the carcasses of slaughtered animals hung from the rafters. The dirt floor was dark and damp in many places. The man pulled out one of his knives and prodded one of the carcasses hanging from a hook.

"The nobles enjoy their fine meals of meat but have no idea how it gets to their tables," said the man as he swatted away some flies. Somewhere outside an animal was braying loudly, as if struggling for its life. The noise stopped abruptly.

"That must have been my brother. He just slaughtered another horse," said the man as he made a motion with his hands across his throat. Yoona shuddered.

The man laughed.

"Did you know my brother and I were once humble farmers from the northern provinces? One day barbarians raided our village and we were their prisoners for three years."

The man cut off a small sliver from the carcass in front of him with his knife. He chewed the raw meat slowly in his mouth.

"To a Korean farmer, a cow is too precious to eat and used only for plowing the fields. The barbarians have a taste for meat and keep herds of sheep and cattle. They use the hide, meat and bones of an animal for everything and even drink the milk of horses," said the man.

The man inspected the slabs of meat before him.

"I learned my butcher's trade from them. It has been quite useful to me."

The man looked over Yoona as if giving her a quick inspection.

"I need some help around this place. A couple weeks of cleaning and fetching water and that bag of bones which looks like a horse is yours," said the man. "Starting now."

Yoona bowed deeply to the man in gratitude. She took

off her sandals and grabbed two water buckets and a pole. Yoona slung the buckets and pole over her shoulders and ran off to a well she had passed by earlier.

The well was at the bottom of a hill. Yoona felt the heavy weight of the loaded buckets on her shoulders as she made her way back up the hill but she did not mind. Yoona didn't know why but she felt energized by her new goal.

The prince had told Yoona his horse was his lifelong companion, a gift from his uncle during happier times in his native land. Yoona imagined the look of surprise and joy on the prince's face when he was reunited with his mount in the future.

Soon Yoona was busy cleaning. The yard was especially foul with animal remains and dirt. Yoona splashed water on the ground and swept up the place. She also ran back and forth with hay for the animals that were kept fenced-off for future slaughter.

Yoona saw that the man with the knives had taken Toki from the herd and placed the horse in a separate corner of the yard. The man was now busy selling cuts of meat from a market stall nearby.

The little boy called Yoona 'big sister' and gave her directions on what needed to be done for the day. The work was harder than what Yoona was used to back home but it wasn't entirely new to her.

The day passed quickly and dinner time approached. Yoona was covered in dirt and sweat.

"I'm impressed. You worked hard for a highborn young lady. You may go now," said the man with a laugh.

Yoona bowed to the man. She retrieved her sandals but did not put them on because her feet were dirty. Yoona walked over to Toki, gave the animal a final pat and left the slaughter yard.

Yoona did not head directly back home. She made her way to the stream Mina had pointed out. After passing through a neighborhood of winding and narrow streets, Yoona found herself on the banks of the stream.

The place was crowded with families. Naked little children cried and played in the water. Women squatted on the banks and pounded clothes with washing stones.

Conversations in Korean spoken with unfamiliar dialects mingled in the air. The people living by the stream had come from all corners of Korea as refugees from the war.

Yoona found a secluded spot near some bushes. She felt herself blushing as she removed her stained clothing. Almost completely naked, Yoona walked into the water holding the bundle of clothing. The water came up to her knees and felt cool compared to the hot summer air. The bottom of the stream was soft and sandy under Yoona's bare feet.

Yoona washed her clothes as best as she could. She then cleaned herself off. Yoona's body ached from working all day but she was happy.

Yoona finally came back home. Her clothes were still damp. Everyone was gathered around the dinner table.

"Where did you go?" asked Yuni.

"So many places, Yuni," said Yoona as she eagerly devoured the food placed before her. She took double servings of everything except for the thinly-sliced pieces of cooked beef the servant had specially prepared. That dish Yoona could not bear to touch.

Chapter 35

Yoona was back at the military camp with her aunt.

The open field where the soldiers rested was cleared. Tents had been erected and provided protection from the elements. The soldiers with the worst injuries had been moved to more comfortable quarters. The healthier soldiers spent their days drinking rice wine and playing dice games with their comrades.

Yoona met up with the prince. When she had shown up with food and medicine, the other soldiers teased the prince and said, "Prince Lee, your pretty beloved is here."

The soldiers near the prince solemnly bowed to Yoona as if she was a royal princess. She blushed deeply. Yoona bowed to the men and offered them rice cakes. The soldiers eagerly pounced on the treats and proclaimed them the best they had ever tasted.

Yoona and the prince finally found some time together as they walked together in a quiet area behind the barracks. The prince told Yoona stories of battles in faraway places and marching for days in rain with no food.

Yoona could almost hear the crashing of swords against armor and the cries of the fallen men in her mind.

The enemy was ruthless and fought hard. Once, the prince and his men had been surrounded on a mountaintop by the enemy.

"I thought for sure I was going to die that day. I thought of my native land where my ancestors are buried. Yoona, I thought of you and the hope I found after coming here to Korea. I then rallied my comrades with a battle cry and we charged the enemy."

"Oh!" said Yoona.

"It was a charge by desperate men with nothing to lose. I was surprised when the enemy fled before our attack."

Yoona and the prince walked together in silence for a while.

"Your family's journey to Hanyang was a safe one?" asked the prince.

"It was a long one," said Yoona. Yoona imagined the prince did not care to hear about all the details of the journey and the events back home that led up to it. The prince had seen many things, braved many dangers and suffered much hardship after all, thought Yoona.

"I feel as though I am blessed by the heavens. I am alive and in one piece. Though I fear I have lost my horse," said the prince.

Yoona kept quiet about Toki. She wanted to surprise the prince when he was fully recovered.

Gomo appeared from behind a building. Yoona had already told her aunt about the prince and his arrival in Hanyang.

"Yoona, it's time to go back home. Hello, Prince Lee. It is good to see you again. You must come stay at the villa in Bukchon after you get better," said Gomo.

"Thank you, I will certainly take up your invitation," said the prince.

As Yoona walked away with Gomo, she looked back over her shoulder at the prince. The prince waved to Yoona. Yoona felt joy in her heart. She and the prince would see each other again in a day or two.

Chapter 36

Yoona was covered head to toe in dirt and sweat. She had worked every day for the past couple weeks at the slaughter yard. Yoona could not count the number of water buckets she had hauled and the ones she carried now seemed to weigh as much as giant rocks.

Yoona was glad the prince couldn't see her now. Whenever Yoona went to see the prince she wore her nicest clothes and even dabbed on herself a little bit of scented water she had made by mixing flower petals with spring water.

The man with the sharp knives came up to Yoona.

"My highborn young lady, you have worked harder than I thought you would. I expected you to give up after a day. Your work here is done, you may take the horse," said the man.

"Thank you so much, kind sir," said Yoona as she bowed deeply to the man.

"No, no, the pleasure is all mine. I have never met such a humble and hard-working noble young lady before," said the man as he fashioned a bridle for Toki out of old rope.

Yoona and the man walked to the corner of the yard where Toki was kept. Every time Yoona came to work at the yard she had brought kitchen scraps from the house to feed Toki.

Toki approached the two. The reins were in Yoona's hands and she and Toki were free to go. Yoona bowed once more to the man and made her way down the hill. Yoona turned around and saw the man and his son standing together and looking at her leaving with Toki.

Yoona made her way to the stream. She was now familiar with the ritual of finding a secluded spot and washing herself.

Yoona quickly slipped out of her outer clothes and went into the water. This time however a crowd of small children came up to Yoona. Many of them were as naked as Yoona.

"Where did you get the horse, unni?"

"How much food does it eat?"

"Can you ride it?"

"How did you get this horse?"

"I hauled many buckets of water and cleaned the stables of the man who owned this horse," said Yoona to the little boy who asked the last question.

"Why?" asked the boy as he looked at the mangy animal.

"Because I want to give it back to a young man I know, a young man who once owned the horse and loved it very much."

"Why?"

Yoona thought about that question for a bit. She hadn't really thought about why she did what she did.

"Because I love the young man very much," answered Yoona.

"Um, okay," said the little boy, looking not wholly satisfied with the answer. Suddenly his attention was diverted by the rest of the children screaming and pointing at a large frog in the stream.

With a splash of water the little boy dashed off to join the other children and catch the critter. Yoona was alone again. She washed her clothes and was soon headed back home with Toki. The sun was setting.

Yoona made her way up the hills of Bukchon. She led Toki to the empty field where the mule was resting. The grass was plentiful here and a nearby ditch was filled with water.

"Good night, Toki," said Yoona as she patted the horse. The animal gently nudged her with his muzzle. "You shall see the prince again," continued Yoona.

Yoona headed to the house in high spirits.

Chapter 37

The next day Yoona and her aunt arrived at the military camp and found the place in chaos. Most of the men were lying on the ground, moaning and clutching their stomachs. Wise old men with medicine bags made their rounds while women rushed back and forth with towels.

"What happened?" Gomo asked one of the women.

"The men ate some tainted food for dinner last night. The medicine men say it will pass in a couple days but meanwhile we must give the sick plenty of water and wet towels."

With that remark, the woman handed Gomo and Yoona a pile of towels. Yoona immediately looked around for the prince.

The prince was lying under a shade tree. After giving

towels to the other men, Yoona turned her attention to the prince. Like the others the prince was groaning with stomach pains. His face was flushed with fever.

"Ah Yoona, you are a sight for tired eyes," said the prince weakly.

"Oh Prince Lee!" cried Yoona. She held the prince's hand. "Please get better soon!"

Yoona folded up a wet towel and put it on the prince's forehead. The prince babbled something incoherent and closed his eyes.

Yoona spent the rest of the day taking care of the others and doing general tasks such as fetching water from a well. From time to time she checked on the prince. The prince fell in and out of a dream-like state throughout the day.

The prince was lying down with his eyes closed as Yoona approached him with a fresh towel. She took the old one off his forehead and started to fold up the new one.

"I missed you so much . . ." said the prince.

"I missed you, too," replied Yoona with a smile.

The prince mumbled something in his native tongue. He switched back to Korean.

"Meet me again at the forked river," said the prince

with a sigh.

Yoona looked over at the prince. His eyes were still closed. Yoona couldn't recall a forked river in her home valley.

"My lovely flower . . . I think your name in Korean means 'beautiful flower?'"

Yoona felt a strange sensation in her stomach, as if she was falling ill. Her name did not mean 'beautiful flower.'

The prince mumbled another female name. Yoona slapped the towel on the prince's head after she was done with it. The prince's eyes fluttered open a little and then closed again.

"Oh!" cried out Yoona. She gathered up her things and walked away.

The rest of the day Yoona worked hard and focused only on her tasks. She checked on the prince a couple more times and felt relieved to find him sleeping. Yoona was calm on the outside but a storm of emotions was brewing inside her. She didn't know how she would react if the prince tried to talk to her.

Finally the day was over and Yoona left with Gomo. The two made their way back home. Yoona grabbed some vegetable scraps from the kitchen to feed Toki and left the house again.

As Yoona walked up to the field, Toki approached her. He gently nibbled the scraps Yoona offered him. The horse was starting to look fatter and healthier. Yoona petted Toki and rested her cheeks against his muzzle.

"Toki, perhaps only you know what's really in the prince's heart?" said Yoona as a tear trickled down her cheek.

Chapter 38

Yoona looked over the military camp. The summer sun bathed everything in a hot and brilliant light. The shade trees that bordered the field were alive with the sound of buzzing cicadas.

Many of the soldiers seemed to be in good spirits. Some of them even had their belongings packed up in neatly-wrapped bundles in front of their tents, as if they were going to leave at a moment's notice.

Yoona had stayed home the last time her aunt came out to help take care of the soldiers, so today was her first time back since she got upset with the prince.

Yoona approached the prince.

"Good afternoon, Yoona," said the prince.

Yoona bowed politely to the prince without a word. She

noticed the prince looked rather handsome. He was freshly shaved and wearing new clothes. The prince was practicing with his sword. He swung the blade in the air.

"I see you are recovered now," said Yoona.

"Yes, I feel much better."

Yoona saw the prince had his own bundle of personal goods.

"Prince Lee, you look as if you're ready to set off on another great journey."

"Those things? It was time to clean up the place."

"A journey through mountains and valleys with forked rivers," continued Yoona.

The prince gave Yoona a puzzled look.

"A journey through new lands with fair young ladies waiting for you."

"Yoona . . ." said the prince. The prince's face was flushed, as if he was becoming agitated. The prince stepped closer. Yoona found herself backing away.

The prince grabbed Yoona's arms. An intense surge of emotion shot through Yoona, a confusing mix of anger and desire. Yoona felt her head spinning. She wanted to surrender to her feelings for the prince . . .

"No," cried out Yoona. She broke away from the prince, turned around and started running.

"Yoona!"

Yoona ran faster and faster.

Yoona ran past the gates of the military field. She ran through the streets of the surrounding neighborhood.

Yoona ran past market stalls and crowds of people. A small dog barked and nipped at Yoona's heels and then gave up the chase. Yoona continued to run until she could run no more. She stood on a street corner and took in big lungfuls of air.

Yoona looked around at her surroundings.

She was in a quiet neighborhood of small shops and market stalls. Little children laughed and played by a dirty pool of water. Two old men were sitting under a tree playing baduk. Rising up in front of Yoona was a large hill known as Namsan, or South Mountain.

A dirt path wound its way into the trees that covered the hill. Yoona felt a sense of comfort as she continued up this path. It was as though she was back in the hills of her home valley. As Yoona made her way up, the dust and noise of the streets below faded away. The only sound was that of birds chirping and the gentle rustling of tree branches.

Yoona finally made it to the top. Her legs and feet felt as heavy as lead. The top of the hill was an open area made of exposed rock.

Yoona found a boulder that looked like a good resting spot and collapsed with exhaustion on the hard surface.

After a while Yoona stirred. She felt a little dizzy. Yoona stood up and took in the view of Hanyang from her perch.

The countless houses in the valley looked tiny from the top of the hill. Yoona had heard that Hanyang was the biggest city in Korea. She thought about all the people squeezed into the land that lay before the Han River.

Yoona wondered how far the Han River flowed before it emptied into the ocean. She had never seen the ocean. The ocean was supposed to be immense and much bigger than any lake.

Yoona had visited a Hanyang fish market once and overheard a fisherman talk about how beautiful the sun looked setting over a calm ocean with no land in sight.

"When the sun started to sink into the horizon it was as though the heavens and the earth had become one," the salty old fisherman said to a woman who worked at the market.

Yoona wondered what the sun looked like setting over the ocean. Yoona remembered the prince had voyaged across the ocean from his native land. The prince had probably seen such a rare sight many times, thought

Yoona.

Thinking of the prince agitated Yoona. She tried to push thoughts of him out of her mind.

Yoona rested some more on the hilltop before she decided to make her way back down. She wasn't sure what time it was. The bright sunlight of noon had faded into the muted light of late afternoon. Yoona slowly made her way down the path, being careful to avoid the sharp rocks.

Yoona made her way up the hills of Bukchon. The sun sank low over the horizon and painted the evening sky in russet-colored pigments.

"Good evening, sir," Yoona bowed to an old man that lived in the neighborhood. By now Yoona was familiar with most of the people in the neighborhood.

Yoona finally arrived at Mina's villa. "Aigoo, what an impulsive young girl you are. Running off like that," said Yoona's aunt when she stepped inside.

"I'm sorry, Gomo," said Yoona as she bowed humbly.

"That's okay. You must be very hungry. Dinner will be ready soon."

The rest of the household was busy. Yoona's father was at a writing table practicing calligraphy. Mina and Yuni were sewing up a quilt together.

Yoona remembered something. She dashed into the kitchen and begged the servant for the vegetable scraps. The servant gathered together a small mound of carrot peelings and lettuce and wrapped it in a piece of cloth. Yoona thanked the servant and left the house again.

Yoona walked to the field up the hill where Toki and the mule grazed. The shadows of the evening twilight seemed to turn the familiar sights of daytime into formless shapes.

The field was soon in Yoona's sights. Yoona stopped in her tracks.

There was a man standing next to Toki.

The man was stroking the horse with one hand and holding his head close to the horse. He was talking to Toki in soft and melodic tones in a foreign language that was at once strange and yet quite familiar to Yoona.

It was the prince.

Yoona walked up slowly to Toki. She did not know what to say to the prince or whether she even wanted to say anything. The horse lifted his head and whinnied when he saw Yoona. Yoona grabbed a handful of vegetable scraps and fed it to Toki.

"Yoona . . ." said the prince. He was situated on one side of the horse and Yoona on the other.

A soft breeze stirred up the humid evening air. The

paper windows of the villas down the hill were lit from inside and the nearby trees buzzed with the sound of summer insects.

"Yoona, I never thought I'd be reunited with my horse again. He was a gift from my uncle."

Yoona continued to feed Toki. The animal gently took the scraps of vegetables in its mouth. The mule trotted up to grab its share of the food.

"Yoona, after I left the valley there were times when I felt all I ever wanted and loved in the world was lost. It's such a crushing feeling to lose all hope, again."

The prince made a move to walk to Yoona's side of the horse. Yoona followed the prince's motions so that the two ended up on different sides of the horse again. Yoona maintained a calm and expressionless demeanor. Yet her heart was pounding.

A long moment of silence passed.

"Yoona, before I left Big Choi told me something that saddened me terribly. He told me he was going to be married to you."

The prince continued, "He said it was already arranged between his family and yours. Big Choi said I was a foreigner with no land or wealth, while his family was the richest in the province."

Yoona remembered she never told the prince the things

Big Choi did to her and her family.

"Yoona, at least let me tell you how much . . ."

"Oh Prince Lee!" Yoona interrupted the prince.

Yoona tried to go around Toki. Excited by Yoona's outburst the horse neighed and blocked Yoona's passage. Yoona stumbled and got up again. She struggled to reach the prince.

The prince held out his hand. His grip was firm and secure. Yoona collapsed into the prince's arms and at that moment heaven and earth seemed to merge into one.

Chapter 39

"Prince Lee, it was so good of you to drop by for dinner last night. It was an unexpected but pleasant surprise. I guess you finally decided to take up my invitation," said Gomo.

The prince was sitting at the breakfast table with the rest of the household. He made eye contact with Yoona and smiled. Yoona gave the prince a shy smile.

"The pleasure is all mine. I have been sleeping too long without a roof over my head. I slept quite blissfully last night," said the prince.

"Yoona has already told you what happened after you left the valley?"

"Yes, I am sorry to hear what happened to the governor.

We can only hope no lasting harm has fallen on him," said the prince.

"I wonder how long this war will continue," said Yoona's father.

"The northerners are very ferocious and war-like. We suffered some major defeats at their hands. But the Korean army has given them a good fight too. It's like two tigers fighting to the death. Both are wounded and trying to deal the other a fatal blow. The Korean king and his generals are planning a new campaign," said the prince.

"Prince Lee, do you have to return to the battlefield?" asked Gomo.

"I swore to serve the Korean king. Whatever he commands, I will obey him," said the prince.

Yoona felt a sinking feeling in her heart. She felt as though her joy was getting snatched away as quickly as she found it. Yoona finished the rest of her meal in silence as everyone else around her laughed and chatted.

Yoona excused herself from the table and went outside.

Yoona walked up the hill. Toki was grazing in the field. Yoona thought the horse looked recovered by now. Toki's muscles were well defined and his coat was shiny and healthy looking.

Yoona pulled out a small carrot she was able to sneak

from the kitchen and offered it to Toki.

"Oh Toki, is there any happiness in this world that is lasting?" said Yoona as she stroked the horse's mane. "Is your master leaving just as soon as he came back into my life?"

The horse silently chewed on the carrot Yoona had offered.

Yoona spotted the prince walking up the hill towards the field. He carried a rolled-up straw mat and ropes under his arm.

"Yoona, would you like to go for a ride?" said the prince as he approached Yoona. He put the straw mat on Toki's back and tied it up with the ropes. The prince took Yoona in his arms and lifted her on top of the horse so she was sitting side saddle. The prince mounted the horse. Soon the prince and Yoona took off on their journey.

"Oh!" exclaimed Yoona as she and the prince rode through a crowded street. It was quite a novel experience sitting high above everyone's heads. Yoona reached out and touched the low-hanging roof of a one-story building as she passed it.

The crowds of people in front of Yoona and the prince parted before the horse. Yoona spotted a muddy puddle in the middle of the street and was glad she didn't have to step in it.

Soon Yoona and the prince were riding through a wide thoroughfare.

The young sons of the nobles galloped up and down the street on their horses, sending little children and adults running for safety. A farmer's wagon stuffed with firewood and pulled by an ox creaked along. A woman riding a chair held aloft by a group of servants passed by. The woman was dressed in fine clothes and wearing a veil but Yoona was able to catch a glimpse of a pale and pretty face.

A ragtag group of children ran alongside the horse and begged the prince for some coins. He reached into his pockets and tossed a couple pieces into the hands of the children.

"The nobleman just gave me the biggest copper coin I have ever seen," shouted one of the children, a barefoot boy with no shirt.

"And the young lady is so pretty, she must be a princess," said another small boy.

Yoona looked around confused. The woman on the chair was gone now, thought Yoona.

A group of soldiers in bright uniforms passed by. Yoona felt her spirits flag at this reminder of the war. The prince could get called any day to join the soldiers. Yoona took the prince's free hand in her own and leaned closer to him.

※

Yoona and the prince rode the horse down another wide road that ran south until it ended at the Han River. Yoona had never seen such a wide river. Small boats floated down the waterway and islands dotted the river at various points.

The prince surveyed the river and directed the horse to a spot on the river bank that was near an island.

"Hold on, Yoona," said the prince.

"Ya!" the prince called out to Toki and suddenly the horse plunged into the water. Water splashed everywhere and Yoona felt her heart skip a beat. Just when Yoona thought she was going to sink into the river the water stopped rising around her knees.

The horse surged against the waves and soon Yoona and the prince made their way to the other side of the river.

Yoona and the prince found themselves back on dry land. Green rice fields stretched before them into the distant mountains. The crowded streets of Hanyang were on the other side of the river now.

Yoona breathed deeply and took in the strong earthy smell of the countryside. The summer air was sticky and humid.

"Ya!" said the prince. The horse gave a spirited neigh and galloped down a dirt road that cut through a rice field. The wind blew through Yoona's hair. The scenery rushed by in a blur and all worries of the uncertain future seemed to melt away.

The prince eventually stopped next to a grassy field. Hanyang was just a dark smudge in the distance and the Han River a pale gray stripe.

The prince dismounted and lifted Yoona off Toki. He patted the horse and whispered softly to him in his native tongue. The horse trotted off to a green patch of grass.

"Prince Lee, what is the name of your horse? You never told me."

"His name in my language means 'Flying Dragon,'" said the prince.

"That's funny because I've been calling him by a completely different name," said Yoona.

"What is that?"

"I've been calling him Toki, which means 'rabbit' in Korean," said Yoona with a sly smile.

The prince laughed. "He does eat a lot of grass like a rabbit. Toki sounds like a good name. I shall call him Toki from now on."

Yoona and the prince walked along a raised dirt path

bordered by a flooded rice field. The path ran until it met another path and then more after that, forming a grid covering the flat and fertile plain. A few scattered farmers were hunched over the fields and pulling weeds. The prince took Yoona's hand in his.

Yoona told the prince of the story of how she found Toki as he was being herded to a slaughter yard. She told the prince of working for the man with the sharp knives in order to buy back Toki from him.

"That was quite selfless of you," said the prince.

Yoona was surprised. She hadn't really thought of her act as being selfless. In fact, Yoona had recently felt guilty because she selfishly wished the prince wouldn't go off back to war.

So what if the northerners were to reach the gates of Hanyang? Yoona wished she and the prince could just keep on riding further and further away into the hills south of Hanyang.

Yoona and the prince walked around back to Toki. The prince lifted Yoona on top of the saddle, mounted the horse himself and soon the two were headed back to Hanyang.

❧

"Prince Lee, I know where we can go," said Yoona as the two rode through the streets of Hanyang. It was late afternoon already.

Yoona remembered the landmarks and streets to follow and soon she and the prince were at the Big Eastern Gate. The two dismounted and the prince gave a copper coin to a boy who was watching over the horses tied up near the market entrance.

Yoona and the prince walked among the crowds of people that thronged the marketplace. The prince's eyes lit up at the sight of the exotic goods and foreign merchants. He stopped by the stall of a Chinese merchant and chatted with the man in his native language.

Yoona and the prince resumed their exploration of the market. The prince would take time to point out to Yoona the origins and uses of various items. Yoona felt a bit awed at the prince's worldly knowledge.

"Prince Lee, you must be well-travelled to know so many things," said Yoona.

"I guess you can say I am well-travelled. I was tossed on the ocean waves and landed on other shores before coming to Korea," said the prince.

The smell of meat cooking over an open fire drifted across the marketplace. Yoona and the prince were in an area of the market filled with stalls selling food and drink. Wooden tables provided a place to sit down and eat.

The prince ordered for Yoona and himself a couple rice

balls and meat cooked on wooden skewers.

Yoona sat on a bench with the prince and ate the simple meal. The numerous cooking fires gave the whole place a smoky smell. Conversations in foreign tongues mingled with the sound of laughter.

The prince was by Yoona's side and he was so close Yoona could feel the warmth of the prince's body. Yoona leaned in closer to the prince and felt joy in her heart. The future was unknown. What was real were the sensations of the present.

The sun was already setting as Yoona and the prince made their way up the hilly streets of Bukchon. The prince led Toki with one hand and held Yoona's hand in the other.

The neighborhood was quiet. The muted sounds of household conversations carried over the walls of the villas. There was a soft knocking sound coming from somewhere, as if someone was using a wooden stick to pound laundry.

The prince led Toki back to the pasture. He gave the horse one final pat. The prince turned to Yoona.

"Yoona, when I first came to these shores I felt I was alone in this world. I had lost everything. Then I met you and it was like a bit of light had come back into my life."

The prince continued, "When I came here to look for

you yesterday and saw my horse, I felt that same feeling of hope for a brighter tomorrow."

"What's the matter, Yoona? Why are you crying?" said the prince as he gently stroked Yoona's cheek.

"Oh, I just got a little something in my eye."

"Tell me what's in your heart, Yoona."

Yoona told the prince how she was so afraid he was going to get called to fight again in the Korean army. "Prince Lee, I feel like just at the moment of my happiness I am losing everything."

The prince paused for a moment as if he was thinking of something.

"Yoona, when I first sailed to your country I noticed the coastline has many islands. Let's go, let's forget about this war, let's sail off into the ocean and find ourselves an island where no one can find us," said the prince.

"I'll go anywhere with you!" said Yoona.

Yoona and the prince embraced each other. The two remained in each other's arms in silence until the prince finally spoke up.

"Well, I must leave now and go back to the barracks. I had to ask leave from my commander to find you," said the prince.

Yoona gave the prince a farewell hug. "Come back soon," she said.

The prince made his way down the hill. Yoona watched his progress until he disappeared around a corner. The evening light was ebbing and Yoona made her way back to the villa.

Chapter 40

Over the next couple days Yoona thought about the prince's proposal to sail off to a distant island.

Yoona wondered what an island surrounded by the ocean looked like. Was it like one of the islands in the Han River, a little sliver of land with vegetation growing on it? Yoona thought those islands didn't look too isolated. In some places along the river a grown man could wade into the water and reach one of the islands.

Yoona remembered back home in the mountains there was a large lake with a wooded island in the middle of it. The local boys competed every summer to swim to it. Many gave up. Even the ones that made it had to rest on the island before swimming back.

None of the girls had the strength to swim to it, so the

boys would tell them the island was a magical place with spirits and talking birds. Yoona often sat on the banks and wished she could explore the island in the middle of the lake.

Yoona remembered something else. She had visited the prince one day at the military camp and saw two soldiers locked up with heavy wooden boards and iron chains around their necks.

The prince told Yoona military discipline was harsh and even high-ranking officers could be locked up, beaten or executed for disobeying orders.

Yoona shuddered. She did not want to see the prince with a heavy wooden board around his neck.

Yoona wondered if it was even possible to live on an island for the rest of her life. She thought she would miss her father and Yuni very much.

Yoona thought it would be good to find an island with another identical island next to it. She and the prince would live on one island while her father and Yuni lived on the other. A small boat could provide transport between the two islands.

Yoona decided wherever the prince wished to go, she would follow him.

Chapter 41

"Yoona, wake up!"

Yoona drifted in and out of sleep. She had been dreaming of an island in the middle of an ocean, or at least what she imagined the ocean to look like. Islands in the ocean had occupied Yoona's thoughts for the past week.

Yoona wiped her eyes and straightened her hair. The natural light inside the bedroom was dim, as if daybreak was just around the corner.

Mina was standing over Yoona. There was a sound of gongs and drums being beaten outside. Yoona wondered who was making such a loud noise so early in the morning.

"Yoona, the war is over! The Korean army defeated the

northerners," said Mina.

"Huh? When?"

"I think it happened about a week ago. A messenger finally brought the news to the king in Hanyang last evening and it just spread overnight like a fire."

Yoona quickly put on some outerwear and stepped outside with Mina.

Yoona and Mina ran up the street. Yoona's father, Yuni and Gomo were already standing at a street corner that was the highest point in the neighborhood. Other neighbors were milling about.

The noises of drums and gongs clamored from the streets at the bottom of the hill. In the distance flashes of light went off with a soft pop as people set off small firecrackers. Shouts of *manseh manseh* carried over the rooftops.

Soon a large group of people was gathered in the street. The morning sun was rising over the mountains to the east. Someone in the crowd shouted *manseh!*

Manseh! Manseh! Ten thousand years!

Yoona joined everyone else in the joyful cheering.

Over a period of several weeks the city of Hanyang seemed transformed after the news of the war's end.

The temples overflowed with crowds that came to offer their prayers of gratitude and the markets were busy as people spent silver that had been long-buried and hidden in the ground. An increased stream of traffic came in and out of the main gates as former refugees from the provinces headed home while endless mule trains brought goods into the city.

The noble families often gathered together for large banquets where wine flowed freely. Yoona's father told her how the war had brought many powerful families from all over Korea together in one place and many of them had taken advantage of the access to the royal family to plot their own advancement.

There were recent rumors of a daughter from a prominent family who had fallen in love with the son of an opposing clan and run off with him, and other such romances filled the gossip of the nobles.

Yoona visited the prince often but he seemed even busier with the end of the war. The prince told Yoona the soldiers had to drill every day for a grand victory parade that was coming up soon. Yoona was carried away by the excitement of it all and couldn't wait.

Chapter 42

Finally the day of the parade arrived. Yoona along with her family and Mina's family was standing among a crowd of other noble families that had gathered at the side of a wide boulevard that ran north and south.

A walled complex of government buildings nearby was the end of the parade route. Further down the boulevard the general population of Hanyang had taken up spaces by the side of the road to watch the parade.

Yoona thought the crowd of ordinary people further down from the nobles was more lively and enjoying a good time. There was a general air of festivity as children laughed and played and the adults drank rice wine and ate food.

The nobles in contrast stood stiffly in their fine clothes.

The noblewomen shielded their faces with veils and the gentlemen fanned themselves to ward off the summer heat.

Silence swept over the crowd. Everyone turned their heads to look down the street in the direction opposite from the government complex.

Far off in the distance a wall of men dressed in bright uniforms was advancing towards the government complex. As the wall of men slowly drew closer a cheer swept through the crowd like a roaring wave.

"The royal guards are approaching," said someone next to Yoona.

With a display of brightly-colored banners and uniforms the royal guard slowly marched past where the nobles stood. The men carried pole axes and short swords.

Yoona counted the column of men as ten men across and ten men deep. The royal guard made their way to the front of the government building complex and lined up at the main gates.

"The royal family is coming up now," said another person.

Everyone kneeled and looked down at the ground. Yoona stole a quick look as the royals passed by. She felt a little disappointed because all she could see was an ornate wooden box large enough to hold a sitting man being carried by about twenty men.

A smaller wooden box passed after the bigger one. Yoona imagined this one carried the queen. Yoona wondered if the royal family members spent their entire lives carried around in wooden boxes and thought it was far better to run around carefree in the hills as she did back home.

The wooden boxes were followed by several chairs, each of them carried by about four men. The chairs had drapes to hide their occupants from public view. At one point a face looked out from behind one of the covered chairs.

"Oh!" exclaimed Yoona to herself because the face was that of a young girl about the same age as her. So that's what a princess looks like, she thought.

The wooden boxes and covered chairs passed through the main gates of the government complex and disappeared inside.

Next came a group of young men on horseback. Some of the horses bucked as their riders tried to keep them under control while others trotted at a walking pace.

Yoona thought the young men looked rather regal with their fine clothes and shiny weapons. She realized the young men were princes of the royal family and felt a little sad because her father told her whenever the reigning king died his sons often fought and tried to kill one other.

Next in line in the procession were the king's ministers. The gray-bearded men looked to be about the same age as Yoona's father and wore the robes and hats of scholars.

In contrast to the spirited princes the ministers carried themselves in a quiet and reserved manner fitting men who advised the king on important affairs and dealt with foreign nations.

The great generals of the Korean army followed the ministers. The generals rode their mounts with a dignified air while their lieutenants marched behind them and carried the colorful battle flags of their respective divisions.

The battle flags flapped in the air and Yoona felt a swelling sense of excitement. One of the flags depicted a fierce dragon while another had a tiger that looked ready to strike its enemies.

"The Prince of Dai Viet is up ahead!" said someone in the crowd.

Yoona's heart fluttered as she stood on her toes to get a better view.

The generals passed by. Soon an old man with a flowing beard riding a magnificent white charger came down the boulevard. He wore a sword by his side and was dressed in a splendid suit of armor.

Yoona realized the old man was *the* Prince of Dai Viet,

the clan head of the Lee family and heir to the throne of Dai Viet before he was overthrown.

Yoona overheard people in the crowd talking about the Prince of Dai Viet:

"Where did he come from?"

"A foreign land to the south of us and across the ocean."

"I heard the Prince of Dai Viet and his men fought bravely in the war against the northern tribes."

"I never met anyone that wasn't from Korea. I wonder what such a person is like."

Yoona wished so much to tell the crowd about the prince of Dai Viet she knew. Perhaps he wasn't *the* Prince of Dai Viet but he was *her* prince of Dai Viet. But Yoona had been raised to not say much in the presence of her elders so she remained silent.

A group of musicians banging on gongs and drums followed the Prince of Dai Viet. Dancers with streamers in their hats twirled their heads and leapt into the air.

The traffic of so many people was raising up clouds of fine dust and the summer sun was now beating down fiercely. The nobles waved their fans faster to fight the heat.

After the musicians and dancers came groups of men on horseback followed by foot soldiers. The foot soldiers in turn were followed by more men on horseback. The soldiers did not follow the royals and the royal guard into the walled complex but instead lined up in orderly rows outside. This pattern repeated itself for a while.

A murmur went through the crowd as the latest group of men on horseback passed by. The men wore armor similar in fashion to that worn by the Prince of Dai Viet.

Yoona felt her heart beating faster as she scanned the faces of the men. Yoona felt her spirits leap when she finally spotted the prince among his countrymen.

Sunlight glinted off the polished surface of the prince's armor and helmet. The prince carried his sword and bow by his side and a quiver of arrows was slung over his back. His horse Toki kicked and pranced as the prince pulled on his reins.

Yoona knew she was one face among many in the crowd but she imagined the prince could see her so she straightened her dress and patted her hair.

Soon the prince passed from view. The column of marching soldiers and men on horseback stretched far down the street. The people cheered and shouted. Yoona felt a leaping joy in her heart as she joined the cheering.

Chapter 43

A few days later Yoona was with her family and Mina's family on a small hilltop that overlooked the Han River. It was evening and numerous paper lanterns lit up a path that twisted its way up the hill. Other families had gathered to watch a spectacle that was to present itself soon.

The prince was by Yoona's side. He told Yoona about meeting the Korean king and the royal feasts that followed the parade. The prince reached into a small sack he carried and offered Yoona a fruit from the feasts. It was a Jeju tangerine.

Yoona peeled the soft skin of the fruit and remembered if she wasn't careful the fruit would squirt juice into her eyes. She offered the prince a piece first and fed him a slice.

Yoona took a piece for herself and bit into the soft fruit. As the sweet juice dripped on her lips Yoona remembered the last time she tasted a Jeju tangerine. She remembered the forested hills and clear skies of the valley she called home . . .

"Look! Here comes the royal procession," someone on the hill shouted.

Everyone's attention turned towards the Han River. A fleet of river boats was making its way down the waterway. Each boat held a festive crowd of people. Flaming torches lit up the boats and cast dancing lights on the river.

Suddenly there was a popping sound followed by a series of rapid explosions.

One of the boats was firing fireworks into the air. Yoona had never seen such a large and elaborate display of fireworks. The bursts of light looked like strange flowers that bloomed in the night sky for one brief glorious moment and then fizzled away. Like life itself, Yoona thought.

Yoona huddled closer to the prince as the two sat on a rock watching the fireworks.

"Yoona, I wanted to tell you the King of Korea met with the Lee clan of Dai Viet yesterday," said the prince.

"He was grateful for our service to Korea in the war against the northerners and granted us land in the northern provinces. Hundreds and hundreds of acres of good farmland," continued the prince.

The prince took Yoona's hand in his own.

"I think it is about a week's journey from your home valley. Yoona, I know you wish to be close to your family but . . ." The prince paused as if he was trying to think of what to say next.

"Prince Lee, remember what I promised you before? I'll go anywhere with you," said Yoona.

"You will? Yes of course, you said you would. Yoona, with you by my side the future seems boundless!" said the prince as he drew Yoona closer to him. The sound of fireworks grew fainter as the boats drifted down the river and away from the hill.

A couple days passed. It was time to head back home.

The servant locked up the villa gates with a cast-iron lock and promised Gomo she would check on it once a week. Two mules loaded with food and household goods waited nearby. Yuni fidgeted and asked her father how long it would take to go back home.

Mina and Yoona sat near the villa walls and talked excitedly about a nobleman's son from Hanyang who had met Mina only a couple days ago. The young man tearfully confessed his love for Mina when he found out she was leaving soon.

The prince walked over to the two girls with Toki following him.

"Now what are you two girls giggling and whispering about?" said the prince with a laugh.

"Matters of the heart, Prince Lee," said Mina.

"Ah Mina, I have a little bit of experience in those things," said the prince.

"Prince Lee, what do you think about long distance love?" said Mina.

"Long distance love?"

"Yes. If two souls are separated by a great distance, is it possible for them to remain true to their feelings for each other?" said Mina.

"Ah! I think if their love for each other is heartfelt then no distance can be too great," said the prince.

"Thank you, Prince Lee. Perhaps you can give us more words of wisdom as we travel back home."

The prince laughed. "Yes, Mina. It's going to be a long journey and I imagine we'll have plenty of time."

Soon the entire group was traveling through the streets of Hanyang. Yoona walked alongside the mules with Mina and Yuni. Gomo was riding Toki side saddle. Yoona's father also rode the horse and the prince walked alongside them.

Yoona felt a little sad as she took in the passing scenery of crowded market stalls and buildings. She wondered if she would ever come back to Hanyang again. Yoona recalled the late evenings when small groups of people in the neighborhoods gathered at street food vendors to eat and drink.

Yoona wondered if the families that had sought refuge at the stream she bathed in had gone back to their home valleys. She remembered how refreshing the water from the stream felt on her body after working all day in the slaughter yard.

A temple bell chimed somewhere in the distance.

Yoona had visited a few temples in Hanyang with her father. She remembered them as quiet and peaceful places. Though the summer sun might beat down like a hammer the interiors of the temples were always cool and dark inside and scented with the sweet smell of incense.

Yoona remembered she tried to avoid creaking the wooden floors of the temples as her father offered a prayer to the Enlightened One. Yoona thought the Enlightened One always looked so serene, as if he knew both the troubles and pleasures of the world were fleeting.

The group passed through a busy farmer's market. Farmers from the surrounding countryside sold their produce in small and large lots. Shrewd mothers inspected individual vegetables while clever men who had never worked in a field eyed giant sacks of rice grains.

The clever men made calculations with little beads and dangled small pouches of silver coins in their pale and soft fingers to make offers on the sacks of rice. Yoona thought the farmers and the clever men were like foxes and badgers. The fox was trying to steal a chicken egg the badger possessed.

A snack vendor was selling dried fish from a small stand. The prince took out a couple coins and bought strips of dried fish for everyone.

Yoona chewed on the tough and chewy meat that had been warmed over a smoky charcoal fire. She realized it was her last taste of Hanyang, this salty taste of the ocean which she had never seen.

The group exited the marketplace and travelled down one of the main boulevards. Ox carts loaded with household goods lumbered down the dusty road. Crowds of people conversing in regional accents mingled on the street corners.

A woman carried on a covered chair by her servants passed by. Yoona thought the noblewomen of Hanyang were quite refined in their speech and dress, like rare blossoms. Yoona felt as though she was a common roadside flower in comparison.

Finally one of the main city gates came into view at the end of the boulevard. The big wooden doors were wide open and traffic was streaming in and out.

Soon Yoona was passing through the gates. She felt a sense of finality, of leaving behind one season of life and entering another as she travelled through the dark tunnel-like interior of the gate and exited back into the sunlit world.

The road that led the way back home through rugged mountains and valleys was up ahead.

Chapter 44

Yoona, the prince and the rest of the group travelled for several days. The trek to Hanyang earlier in the year had taken a rugged and dangerous route through the hills and mountains because of necessity. In contrast the journey back home stayed mostly on the main roads with occasional forays into the hills.

The country roads were packed with families making the journey back to their hometowns. Groups of ex-soldiers marched along the roads singing songs of lost sweethearts and returning to distant homes. It seemed as though the entire population of Korea was on the move.

Outside a small village Yoona saw a mother collapsing and crying at the sight of her son returning from the battlefield unharmed.

There were signs of destruction too. Once, Yoona's father pointed out to her a hilltop that was bare and stripped of trees. A couple of stones and charred timbers were all that remained of a temple that once stood there.

Some areas were completely devoid of any signs of human habitation. Thick grass grew where rice fields once stood and saplings sprouted in the yards of empty houses.

In other areas the people were busy rebuilding and replanting. The valleys echoed with the crashing sounds of trees getting chopped down and cut into building materials. Rows of freshly-made clay and mud bricks sat under the summer sun. Farmers were out in the fields with shovels digging out damaged irrigation ditches.

After each day's journey the group often stayed at a roadside inn or camped out in the hills under the shelter of the trees. Yoona felt quite safe and comfortable with the prince nearby on these occasions, even when he sometimes snored.

One day after an entire day of traveling the group was passing through a quiet mountain valley when a gentleman on horseback rode up beside them.

The gentleman looked a bit older than Yoona's father, with a white beard and a sad face. The gentleman nodded politely to Yoona's father, recognizing him as a fellow gentleman scholar.

"Where are you headed?" asked the gentleman.

Yoona's father told him the group was headed back home from Hanyang.

"The sun will set soon. Do you have a place to stay overnight? If not, I welcome you as a guest," said the gentleman.

Yoona's spirits rose at the thought of spending the night in a clean futon under a roof. The rest of the group seemed cheered by the idea too and thanked the gentleman for his hospitality.

The gentleman lead the way and soon the group found itself in sight of a grand country estate. It was about the same size as Mina's place back home. Several buildings appeared to be damaged from the war, with burnt-out roofs and collapsed walls.

The entire group was seated inside a spacious dining room with the gentleman at the head. A couple servants ran back and forth with plates of food and pots of tea.

Yoona thought the place felt oddly empty and quiet. She wondered where the rest of the gentleman's family members were.

"Prince Lee, I understand you come to Korea from a foreign land," said the gentleman.

The prince nodded and told the gentleman the story of his family's defeat and escape from his native country.

"I heard the story of your people's heroism and service to the Korean king," said the gentleman.

The prince told the gentleman about the grant of land by the king to his family.

"Splendid! So you shall make Korea your new home. In a generation the Lee family will become known as one of the great families of Korea."

The prince smiled. "My desires are simple. I only wish to farm the land and raise a family and live in peace."

The gentleman looked at once sad and serious. "We can only hope for peace. War unfortunately is a fact of life in our land, as certain as the sun rising and rain falling."

The gentleman pulled up a small writing table that was behind him. He took a brush and a piece of scrap paper and rapidly drew a rough sketch. He showed it to the prince.

Yoona craned her neck to get a better look. The ink was still glossy and wet on the paper. The gentleman had drawn a sort of map: a large landmass with a peninsula sticking out of it like the snout of an animal and a chain of islands to the east of the peninsula.

"This is our land," said the gentleman as he pointed to the peninsula. He continued, "Here is the Middle

Kingdom of the Chinese and the war-like tribes to the north." The gentleman was pointing at the large landmass.

"And finally here lies the land of the rising sun," he said pointing to the chain of islands in the ocean.

"To wish for peace is almost futile. Whatever great power controls the Korean peninsula controls this entire region," said the gentleman as he made a sweeping gesture with his hand over the map.

The gentleman set the map down. "I have lost my entire family to this recent war. My three sons and my wife."

Everyone at the table looked down at their food. Yoona thought the gentleman's story was quite tragic. Now she knew the reason for the strange emptiness of the place.

The gentleman spoke up again, "But please, let's eat and drink and be happy. I feel a sense of hope for the future when I hear a story like yours, Prince Lee. From great loss comes a new beginning."

Soon everyone was laughing and chatting and enjoying the good food the gentleman had served. After dinner the men and Gomo played baduk while Yuni and Mina played with a small dog owned by the gentleman.

Yoona in the meantime explored the multiple rooms that made up the gentleman's estate. The rooms were connected to each other with sliding paper doors. Each room was modestly furnished with woven floor mats and a couple pieces of furniture.

Yoona found herself in what appeared to be a woman's room. A lacquer jewelry box and hand mirror sat on a table, as if the owner had just momentarily left them.

A stringed Korean musical instrument and flute was in the corner of the room. Yoona imagined the mistress of the house to have been a beautiful noblewoman who was also quite talented in the musical arts.

After leaving the woman's room Yoona entered a room with a folding screen that took up an entire wall.

The folding screen depicted three young men on horseback with bows and arrows hunting wild boar. The artist was skilled and had painted the young men looking similar yet different from each other, as if brothers.

Yoona felt as though she was in a forest. She imagined hearing the rustling of branches as the wild boars dashed through the undergrowth, followed closely by the young men.

Yoona was about to enter another room filled with books when Gomo called out to her, "Yoona, where are you?" Gomo's voice was distant, as if she was at the other end of the house.

Yoona rushed through the young men's room and the

woman's room and down a long corridor. She finally ended up in a guest room.

Fresh futons were on the floor. Mina and Yuni were already tucked into bed. Yoona felt as though she had just exited another world and re-entered the world of the living. She was glad to be back in this world.

Yoona's aunt extinguished the lights. Yoona settled into the futon and soon she was asleep.

The next morning found the mules loaded up and ready to travel. The gentleman stood outside the walls of his estate with his household servants. Yoona's father, the prince and Gomo exchanged final farewells with the gentleman. Yoona along with the other girls bowed to the gentleman in unison. Soon the group was making its way down a path that led to the main road.

Chapter 45

After an entire day's traveling, the group slept under the stars and set off again the next morning. Yoona thought the terrain was starting to look familiar. She felt as though she had been in the area before.

Yoona looked up at the fog-shrouded mountains and wondered if a certain hidden valley was somewhere close by. Yoona's memories of that valley were coming back . . .

"We made it! I see the Old Man Mountain," said Yuni excitedly as she pointed at a local landmark, an exposed rock on a hill that looked like the craggy face of an old man.

Yoona realized why the place looked so familiar. It was home. Yoona finally recognized the outlines of the mountains and hills she had explored countless times.

"Oh! I know a shortcut to the valley," said Yoona as she guided everyone up a familiar path that went up a large hill before descending into the valley. The group followed her lead and hiked up the narrow path.

Halfway up the path the group encountered a roadblock. Yoona froze but then realized with relief it was long abandoned. Tall grass grew among the fallen trees that blocked the path.

Yoona led the group around the roadblock and further up the mountain. The group finally reached the crest of the mountain.

Yoona felt a wave of emotion choke her. The place she had called home for her entire life lay before her. From a distance the rice fields in the valley looked like a carpet of moss and the orchards were bursting with the lush foliage and green fruits of late summer.

The group carefully made its way down the narrow and rocky path. Mina's family estate was up ahead. Numerous workers were coming in and out of the front gates. Stacks of fresh lumber and building materials were piled outside the walls.

One of the household servants, an older woman, had just exited the front gates when she stopped in her tracks. She squinted in the sun at the group standing before her.

"Aigoo! It's Mina and her mother!" the woman exclaimed and dropped the basket of laundry she had been carrying.

Gomo, Mina and the woman hugged each other. Yoona recognized the woman as a servant who had taken care of Mina since she was a small child.

After much crying and exclamations of *aigoo* among the three females, the servant assumed a more formal manner and bowed politely to the prince and Yoona's father.

The woman called for another servant to take care of the mules and Toki. She led the group past the front gates and into the estate.

"How is the governor doing?" asked Gomo.

"He's . . . recovering," said the servant woman.

Carpenters and other workmen were busy fixing up the place. Many of the buildings had missing doors and gaping holes in their roofs. Piles of smashed tiles and pottery were scattered about the courtyards.

The servant led the group to an inner courtyard. The tiled-roof building where Mina's father had overseen important matters was here.

The group waited near the inner courtyard gates as the servant woman went inside the tiled-roof building. After a while she emerged again with a white-bearded man on her arms. She carefully supported him as he shuffled outside.

It was Mina's father.

"Appa!" said Mina as she rushed to her father. Gomo was right behind her daughter.

Yoona and her family and the prince waited in the shadows as the tearful family reunion unfolded. Mina's family collapsed together into one pile in the courtyard. Mina and her mother sobbed uncontrollably. Mina's father held her and stroked her hair. "Everything is okay now," said Mina's father.

Everyone was gathered together around the dining table at Mina's family estate. A midday meal was spread out before them. Yoona thought the food was quite delicious.

After being away from home so long, Yoona recognized the unique flavors of the local dishes. A soup similar to one commonly served in Hanyang was made with larger dumplings. Another dish used different proportions of local vegetables.

Mina's father's hands trembled slightly as he picked up a tea cup.

"So many things happened here after you and your family left," Mina's father said to Yoona's father. He proceeded to tell the story of Big Choi:

After Yoona's family escaped from the valley, Big Choi

forbade the villagers from leaving and permanently blocked off all the roads. The only way in and out of the valley was through the gates of the long wall that Big Choi's family had built.

Whoever controlled the wall controlled the entire region. The northerners recognized the strategic value of the wall and its fortified gates that sat between two mountains and brought more warriors to the valley. Big Choi sped up construction on his family estate by forcing the local farmers to labor for him.

When Big Choi's estate was finished, it resembled a fortress more than a family estate. A deep moat surrounded it. The high walls of the estate were made of stone and equipped with battlements. The largest building behind the walls was rumored to hold a pit-like dungeon for anyone that dared oppose Big Choi.

Mina's father the governor was too respected a person for Big Choi to toss into his dungeon. But Big Choi often came over and reminded him he was now the master of the valley. He boasted his own father had taken over the capital city of Kaesong.

Once, Big Choi locked up Mina's father with a wooden board and chains around his neck and made him stand outside the gates of his own estate. The locals bowed their heads and looked at the ground as they passed by the old governor.

Big Choi collected more than half the entire rice harvest of the valley on behalf of the northerners. The northerners took the pigs and cows of the farmers for themselves and trampled the fields with their horses.

Soon the villagers were going without food for days at a time. Big Choi and his group of young boys patrolled the village streets and enforced a curfew. Even stray dogs were beaten.

One day a large Korean army arrived and fought the northerners on a plain just outside the long wall. The battle raged for many days. Big Choi forced the farmers to make repairs to the wall and reinforce the defenses. Eventually the Korean army breached the gates and attacked Big Choi's fortified estate.

The defeated northerners fled. The last time someone saw Big Choi he was on the rooftop of his burning estate, screaming and waving his sword. Others thought he escaped to the north.

✻

"Since the battle against the northerners, we have been rebuilding the damage left by the war," said Mina's father after he finished the story. He winced with pain as he rubbed his joints.

The prince recalled he heard of the battle while he was

fighting in a different part of the kingdom. "It was an important victory. The news of it travelled fast," said the prince.

Soon the meal was finished. Yoona and her family had not yet been to their house yet. The mules were left behind at Mina's estate and Yoona's family made their way to the house with the prince and his horse Toki.

As Yoona and her family walked through the village, the little children cried out, "Teacher Chang and his family are back!" The old women exclaimed *aigoo* at the sight of Yoona's family and the men bowed their heads with respect.

Finally the outside walls of the house came into sight. Yoona felt joy welling up inside her. This house was the place where she had been born, the area bounded by the four walls her universe when she was growing up.

The wooden doors of the front gate opened with a creak as Yoona's father pushed against it. A piglet squealed and tried to escape to the outside world. The prince caught the animal in time as it ran out of the open doorway.

A series of grunts indicated the presence of more pigs behind the walls of the house. Yoona held her sister's hand and followed her father and the prince into the courtyard of the house.

The central courtyard was a mud hole occupied by a family of pigs, two grown ones and numerous piglets snorting and squealing as they scurried around the place.

Tall grass grew around the walls of the house and many of the paper screen doors were ripped and broken. Startled sparrows flew out of the thatched roof. In one section the roof was sagging and almost collapsed.

Yoona looked inside what used to be her and Yuni's bedroom. Water had leaked in from the roof and puddled on the floor. A wooden chest looked as though it had been rained upon many times. The blankets and clothing Yoona had left behind were torn to shreds by the pigs.

Well, we're finally home, thought Yoona to herself.

A couple days later the farmer who had used the house as a pig pen apologized to Yoona's father.

"Teacher Chang, I now have eleven children to feed and the northern barbarians burned my crops. So I had to raise some pigs. And I had no news of your family's fate. Did you not say that nothing should ever go to waste?" said the farmer.

Yoona's father nodded in agreement. "Yes, I understand. In these times of want, those who have should give to those who are lacking," said Yoona's father.

The farmer bowed to Yoona's father in gratitude and promised him a couple eggs from his chickens the next time the two met.

Chapter 46

Late summer turned into early autumn. The farmers of the valley were busy preparing for the harvest and repairing their houses.

The prince threw himself into the task of repairing Yoona's home, working from dawn to dusk on things such as patching the roof. He explained to Yoona that his travels on an oceangoing boat had taught him to fix almost anything.

Mina's family estate was almost completely rebuilt by now. Carpenters and stonemasons had come from afar to make the repairs. Soon the governor once again sat inside the tiled-roof building and received visitors from all corners of the province.

There was talk that in addition to the regular harvest

festivities a special celebration at the governor's estate for the entire village was being planned. Yoona wondered if it would be as grand as the one from more than a year ago, when times were peaceful and life seemed simpler.

One day Yoona's father called her into his study room. His expression was calm yet serious, as if he had an important matter to discuss with Yoona.

"Yoona, as you recall I have discussed this matter with you before. You are now of an age to be married."

"Yes, appa," said Yoona.

Back in those days marriage was considered not a matter of the heart but a pragmatic sort of union arranged by the respective parents of the young couple. A good Korean parent would find a suitable match based on the social status and wealth the other side brought to the table. The true wishes or desires of the would-be couple were not important.

"There is a young man who has asked me for your hand in marriage," said Yoona's father. He maintained his formal manner.

"Yes, appa," said Yoona.

"In considering a partner for marriage, one must not be misled by fleeting passions. Rather, one must consider the true character of the person," continued Yoona's father.

Yoona's father paused as if to let the gravity of the matter sink in.

"Yoona, I think this suitor of yours is of noble character and a good match for you. I agree to the union."

"Appa, you have my gratitude for approving this suitor. But will I have occasion to meet the young man?" asked Yoona. Yoona sat with her knees touching the floor with her back straight and hands folded on her lap. Yoona's manner was as formal as her father's.

A hint of a smile crossed Yoona's father's face. "Yoona, you might possibly know this young man. He comes from a foreign land but has learned our customs and manners and served our nation heroically."

"Oh appa! Yes, of course I know him and I love him so much," said Yoona as she reached over and hugged her father. Yoona's father's reserved manner crumbled under his daughter's affections.

"I think sometimes two hearts know what is best for each other better than anyone else," said Yoona's father with a smile.

Yoona's father walked over to a wooden chest in the corner of the room.

"Your aunt wanted to give you something," said Yoona's father as he opened the chest.

Yoona looked inside the chest and gasped.

Inside the chest were several bolts of Chinese silk cloth, the same impossibly soft and shimmering material Yoona had seen at the market in Hanyang. Yoona had never imagined she would wear a dress made of this material. She reached into the chest and touched the material with her fingertips.

"Yoona, why don't you see which color silk suits you best?" continued Yoona's father.

The silk seemed to flow like water as Yoona held it in her hands. The material felt like nothing Yoona had ever touched, as soft as a butterfly's wings.

Chapter 47

A few days later the harvest season arrived. The flooded rice fields of summer were now dry and a golden color. Groups of farmers were out in the fields with their sickles, harvesting the grains. Picture-perfect autumn days replaced the heat and humidity of summer.

Yoona visited Mina's house almost every day for a week so that she could be measured and fitted for the dress. A servant woman who was an expert seamstress fussed over Yoona and draped the Chinese silks on Yoona to find the best fit for her.

One day Gomo noticed Yoona's hands were roughened from the work she did around her father's house. Yoona's aunt brought out a bowl of warm water and a pumice stone.

"Yoona, you must look pretty for your wedding day. I will tell your father you must not to do any hard labor around the house," said Gomo as she rubbed Yoona's hands with the pumice stone.

"But appa needs my help, Gomo," Yoona protested.

"Ah my child, you are surely the apple of your father's eye. But you must listen to me on this matter," said Yoona's aunt.

Yoona walked outside with her aunt as she went to fetch some more water. Servants led mules loaded with supplies through the front gates.

Gomo gave Yoona a warm embrace. "Yoona, we are so happy for you. I wanted to tell you the governor thought your wedding would be a good occasion to celebrate the return of peace to the valley. The wedding celebration will be held right here and it will be a very special one."

Yoona realized the reason for all the preparations at Mina's family estate. She felt joy in her heart and couldn't wait until the day of the wedding.

The harvest was soon brought in and the fields were reduced to stubble and bare dirt. It was time to thresh the grains. Both the farmers and their wives participated in this task. Tawny clouds of dust from the grains hung in the air as the farmers beat bushels of rice against straw mats.

While their parents worked in the fields the children of the farmers swarmed the apple orchards in the hills. The trees groaned with the weight of all the fruit hanging from their branches and the children seemed quite happy to relieve the trees of their burden.

Yoona's father had agreed with Gomo's advice to keep Yoona away from hard labor. The only activity Yoona could still enjoy was going into the hills to find roots and herbs.

Yoona felt so happy whenever she was exploring the mountainside forests she had known since childhood. She knew which hill yielded the best medicinal roots and when to pick the ripe berries before the birds got to them.

Yoona often found herself on the hillside that overlooked Mina's family estate. Mina's place was busy every day with servants running around preparing for the upcoming festivities. A number of visitors from outside the valley had already shown up.

Yoona wondered where all the visitors had come from. She realized the wedding wasn't just about her and the prince but a celebration of hope for a brighter future.

Chapter 48

"Now hold still, Yoona," said Gomo as she applied a dab of red pigment to Yoona's lips. Gomo handed Yoona a hand mirror of polished metal. Yoona, like most Koreans of that time, had rarely seen such a precious object. It was like holding in the palm of one's hand the reflection from the surface of a pond.

Yoona was surprised by the girl that stared back at her in the mirror, she was almost like a different person.

The girl in the mirror had a small face and resembled both Yoona's aunt and her own sister Yuni. Her hair was elaborately arranged and adorned with a hairpin of precious metal.

Yoona smiled at the image in the mirror and saw a small dimple form in the corner of her cheek.

"Yoona, let's see how the dress looks on you," said

Gomo. The seamstress who had stitched together the Chinese silk into a dress carefully unwrapped a large bundle. Everyone in the room let out a soft *ahhh* at the sight of the brightly-colored fabric emerging from behind the plain cotton wrapping.

The seamstress instructed Yoona to hold still and raise her hands over her head. Yoona felt her face flushing because she was dressed only in a cotton undergarment and everyone in the room was looking at her.

The seamstress and Gomo hovered over Yoona. Yoona felt the soft silk enveloping her body as the two women dressed her.

Yoona moved her arms and the fabric rustled softly like leaves on a forest floor. The seamstress pinned together a couple loose flaps and tightened the sash.

"*Wah.* You look so pretty, unni," said Yuni.

The hand mirror was too small to show Yoona the full length of the dress. She couldn't see it but Yoona felt bodily transformed, as if she was a gosling with downy feathers grown up into a creature with splendid plumage.

Gomo and Mina led Yoona out of her father's house and into the courtyard. It was a perfect day in autumn. The sky was clear and a brisk breeze stirred up the freshly fallen leaves inside the courtyard.

Yoona felt everything adorning her was so perfectly put together she dare not trip and fall. She walked with baby steps across the courtyard. Two servants from Mina's household bowed and opened the doors of the front gate.

Yoona was startled at the sight before her eyes. The entire village was waiting outside. A joyful shouting went up from the crowd of farmers and wives and children gathered around the front gates.

On the ground in front of Yoona was a covered chair like the ones she had seen in Hanyang, always occupied by a highborn lady. It was carved out of fine wood and covered with rich fabrics. Gomo and Mina helped Yoona into the chair.

Yoona felt a sensation of rising into the air as Mina's household servants lifted up the chair with wooden poles on both ends. A group of farmers with gongs and drums took up positions ahead of Yoona. Several servants from Mina's house held aloft bright banners that flapped in the wind.

There was a loud noise from a gong and soon the procession was on its way. The farmers banged their drums and laughing village children ran alongside Yoona. Yoona felt as though she was on a boat as the chair swayed and rocked from the motion of the men carrying it.

The familiar landscape of fields and farmhouses passed

before Yoona's eyes. Yoona looked around at the surrounding mountains. The trees were already wearing the fiery shades of autumn.

Yoona thought about the plants that bloomed and died every year and came back to life in the springtime. The individual trees might die but the forests in the mountains seemed destined to go on forever.

Or at least a long time, thought Yoona.

Mina's estate came into view. Yoona felt flush with anticipation as the procession drew closer to the front gates. The procession finally stopped in front of the gates. Yoona felt herself getting lowered back to the ground. Gomo and Mina took Yoona's hands and helped her out of the chair.

"Now hold your hands together in front of you," said Gomo to Yoona. "Take small steps, as if you're walking on eggshells."

Yoona took a deep breath and walked through the front gates.

A murmur rose up from the crowd of nobles gathered inside Mina's family estate. Yoona stole a glance or two at the crowd and tried to find a familiar face. All of the adults looked important and dignified. Yoona's arms started to tremble slightly.

"Umma, is she a princess?" a little child asked her mother.

Yoona smiled when she heard that remark and felt a little less nervous as she walked across the courtyard.

In front of Yoona was a monk tapping on a wooden gourd and behind her was Gomo, Mina and Yuni. Servants walked ahead waving colorful banners. Yoona walked through another courtyard and spotted a familiar figure.

Yoona's heart leapt with joy. The prince was waiting for Yoona at the other end of the central courtyard, in front of the tile-roofed building. Yoona felt the trembling in her arms coming back again and she was glad her arms were covered in silk sleeves.

Yoona remembered what Gomo told her and took small steps across the courtyard. She noticed for the first time that the central courtyard had a stone path running across it from the gate to the tiled-roof building. Yoona could feel the individual stones through the thin fabric of her slippers.

Yoona finally found herself about an arm's length away from the prince. The prince was wearing a fine robe of silk and a crown-like hat and held his arms together in front of him in the same formal manner as Yoona.

The prince made eye contact with Yoona and gave her

only a faint smile because the occasion was very solemn. Yet the prince's dark eyes seemed to smolder and burn.

Yoona wondered if the prince was feeling the same feelings that seemed to overwhelm her, feelings so intense it felt like a fire threatening to consume a house.

The monk started to chant as he tapped his wooden gourd.

Yoona and the prince bowed to each other in a formal manner as if meeting for the first time.

Yoona stood next to the prince and together they bowed, first to the heavens and then to their ancestors. The prince's ancestors were resting somewhere far across the ocean and thus Yoona and the prince bowed south toward the mountains and the distant sea.

Yoona and the prince shared a small bowl of rice wine. Yoona had never tasted rice wine before. She felt her body warming up from the drink.

Yoona looked over at the prince and her gaze met the prince's.

Yoona thought about the prince fleeing from his native land. Now the prince was next to Yoona, so close to her it was as if Yoona and the prince were one. Just then a flock of wild geese flew overhead, headed somewhere south for the winter.

Yoona wondered if it was true geese paired for life.

Yoona remembered as a child seeing a goose with a broken wing helplessly hopping around on the ground while its mate refused to leave its side. Later that day a farmer chased away the healthy goose and killed the injured one. The farmer had to feed his family but Yoona felt sad for the goose that lost its mate.

The monk lit up an incense stick. An aromatic scent filled the air.

Yoona and the prince were now one under heaven.

The servants at Mina's estate lit torches as the autumn light grew dim. After the ceremony Yoona and the prince had greeted so many guests she felt as though all the faces had become one big blur.

Yoona was seated with the prince on a covered platform. A small table in front of them was spread out with arrangements of fruits and rice cakes. The guests were seated at long tables and already feasting.

"Yoona, we're both so happy for you," said Mina as she walked up to where Yoona was seated. A young man was by Mina's side.

"I am Woori Kim from Hanyang. My father had some business with the governor and . . . and that's the reason why I'm here," said the young man.

The young man appeared a bit flustered. He gave a

quick bow and retreated to one of the tables with Mina.

"Prince Lee, that was the young man from Hanyang who likes Mina," said Yoona.

"Ah! So their feelings for each other remained true after all this time and distance apart," said the prince.

"Yes," said Yoona. "Isn't that so wonderful?"

"I know a girl whose heart is so true I think even if I journeyed across the ocean again I would never find another one like her," said the prince.

"Who . . ?" said Yoona before she realized the prince was talking about her. The prince held Yoona's hand underneath the table.

Fireworks went off outside the estate walls and the sounds of laughter carried over from the other courtyards where the villagers were gathered.

Yoona had experienced these sensations before. She remembered just a year ago the prince and his people were newly arrived from their faraway kingdom. Just a year ago, thought Yoona. And yet everything was changed.

Chapter 49

Winter came and went. It was early spring and the fields were still barren. The sky was gray like iron. The chilly air stung Yoona's cheeks whenever the wind picked up.

Yoona was standing with the prince in front of her father's house. Gathered before her was her family and Mina's. More than a few curious villagers were also there. Toki was loaded with household goods and waiting nearby.

"Unni, please visit often," said Yuni as she hugged her sister. Yuni was almost as tall as her older sister now.

"How long will the journey take?" Yoona's father asked the prince.

"We will travel four or five days north before reaching the lands granted by the Korean king to my people," said the prince.

"Ah! The two of you will be arriving just in time to settle down and start the spring planting. Be careful, bandits sometimes travel these roads."

The prince tapped the hilt of his sword. "I will defend my love with all my strength and courage."

"Prince Lee, you have already proven yourself to be brave and honorable. That I don't doubt," said Yoona's father. The prince bowed to Yoona's father.

Yoona embraced her father.

"Appa, please be well and take care of yourself," Yoona cried softly as a tear rolled down her cheek.

Yoona's father laughed gently. "Don't worry, I'll be okay. I'll be busy with a new project of mine writing up a history of these rather interesting times we live in. When you and the prince visit next year you can read whatever is finished."

It was time to go. Yoona and the prince bowed once more to everyone that was gathered. The prince took Yoona by the waist and her lifted her up onto Toki. Soon the three were on the path leading the way out of the village.

Yoona took one last look at the valley and the hills she had called home for her whole life. Once again she was setting off on a long journey but it was one full of hope and anticipation of a new beginning.

Afterword

When Yoona's father captivated her with the legend of Princess Hwang-ok, over eight hundred years had already passed since the Korean epoch of heroic mythology. An almost equal span of time separates us from Yoona and her story of love and courage. Yet it is at once timeless and true.

In the year 1226 Prince Ly Luong Tuong left what is now modern day Vietnam with his extended family and other nobles after a rival faction seized the throne of his kingdom. After many months at sea Prince Ly ended up in the Korean peninsula.

Shortly afterwards, the Mongols invaded the Goryeo kingdom that ruled the Korean peninsula. Prince Ly and his men fought many battles on behalf of his adopted home and people.

After peace returned to the land a grateful Korean king granted Prince Ly and his clan a landholding in northern Korea.

Prince Ly became known as Hwasan Lee.

Today, Prince Ly's descendants number in the thousands and live scattered throughout the Korean peninsula. If you should happen to meet one of them, he or she will be quite happy to tell you the founding legend of the Hwasan Lee clan from Vietnam. And that is a true story.

Dear Reader,

Thank you very much for taking the time to read *A Prince of Vietnam in Korea*. I hope you enjoyed this tale of love, adventure and heroism.

As an author I enjoy hearing from my readers. I can be reached at danee.choi.writer@gmail.com.

Finally, I would greatly appreciate it if you can take some time to share your thoughts about this book on sites such as Amazon and iTunes Books. Your review does not have to be glowing or 5-stars because I appreciate any feedback!

Danee Choi
Seoul, Korea

Made in USA - North Chelmsford, MA
1116570_9780986213755
05.27.2020 1747